PENGUIN BOOKS

HOW I LIVE NOW

Praise for *How I Live Now*

'A crunchily perfect knock-out of a debut novel'
– *Guardian*

'This is a powerful novel: timeless and luminous'
– *Observer*

'That rare, rare thing, a first novel with a sustained,
magical and utterly faultless voice' – Mark Haddon,
author of *The Curious Incident of the Dog
in the Night-Time*

'Intense and startling . . . heartbreakingly romantic'
– *The Times*

'A wonderfully original voice' – *Mail on Sunday*

'Readers won't just read this book, they will let it
possess them' – *Sunday Telegraph*

'It already feels like a classic, in the sense that you
can't ir   an

Books by Meg Rosoff

HOW I LIVE NOW

JUST IN CASE

WHAT I WAS

THE BRIDE'S FAREWELL

THERE IS NO DOG

PICTURE ME GONE

megrosoff.co.uk

MEG ROSOFF

HOW I LIVE NOW

PENGUIN BOOKS

PENGUIN BOOKS

Published by the Penguin Group

Penguin Group (USA) Inc., 375 Hudson Street, New York, New York 10014, USA
Penguin Group (Canada), 90 Eglinton Avenue East, Suite 700, Toronto, Ontario,
Canada M4P 2Y3 (a division of Pearson Canada Inc.)
Penguin Ireland, 25 St Stephen's Green, Dublin 2, Ireland (a division of Penguin Books Ltd)
Penguin Group (Australia), 707 Collins Street, Melbourne, Victoria 3008, Australia
(a division of Pearson Australia Group Pty Ltd)
Penguin Books India Pvt Ltd, 11 Community Centre, Panchsheel Park,
New Delhi – 110 017, India
Penguin Group (NZ), 67 Apollo Drive, Rosedale, Auckland 0632, New Zealand
(a division of Pearson New Zealand Ltd)
Penguin Books (South Africa) (Pty) Ltd, Block D, Rosebank Office Park, 181 Jan Smuts
Avenue, Parktown North, Gauteng 2193, South Africa

Penguin Books Ltd, Registered Offices: 80 Strand, London WC2R 0RL, England

penguin.com

First published 2004
This edition published 2013
001

Copyright © Meg Rosoff, 2004
Extract of *Picture Me Gone* copyright © Meg Rosoff, 2013
All rights reserved

The moral right of the author has been asserted

Set in Adobe Sabon
Printed in Great Britain by Clays Ltd, St Ives plc

British Library Cataloguing in Publication Data
A CIP catalogue record for this book is available from the British Library

ISBN: 978-0-141-34656-4

www.greenpenguin.co.uk

MIX
Paper from
responsible sources
FSC® C018179
www.fsc.org

Penguin Books is committed to a sustainable
future for our business, our readers and our planet.
This book is made from Forest Stewardship
Council™ certified paper.

For Debby

Part One

One

My name is Elizabeth but no one's ever called me that. My father took one look at me when I was born and must have thought I had the face of someone dignified and sad like an old-fashioned queen or a dead person, but what I turned out like is plain, not much there to notice. Even my life so far has been plain. More Daisy than Elizabeth from the word go.

But the summer I went to England to stay with my cousins everything changed. Part of that was because of the war, which supposedly changed lots of things, but I can't remember much about life before the war anyway so it doesn't count in my book, which this is.

Mostly everything changed because of Edmond.

And so here's what happened.

Two

I'm coming off this plane, and I'll tell you why that is later, and landing at London airport and I'm looking around for a middle-aged kind of woman who I've seen in pictures who's my Aunt Penn. The photographs are out of date, but she looked like the type who would wear a big necklace and flat shoes, and maybe some kind of narrow dress in black or grey. But I'm just guessing since the pictures only ever showed her face.

Anyway, I'm looking and looking and everyone's leaving and there's no signal on my phone and I'm thinking Oh Great, I'm going to be abandoned at the airport so that's two countries they don't want me in, when I notice everyone's gone except this kid who comes up to me and says You must be Daisy. And when I look relieved he does too and says I'm Edmond.

Hello Edmond, I said, nice to meet you, and I look at him hard to try to get a feel for what my new life with my cousins might be like.

Now let me tell you what he looks like before I forget

because it's not exactly what you'd expect from your average fourteen-year-old what with the CIGARETTE and hair that looks like he cut it himself with a hatchet in the dead of night, but aside from that he's exactly like some kind of mutt, you know the ones you see at the dog shelter who are kind of hopeful and sweet and put their nose straight into your hand when they meet you with a certain kind of dignity and you know from that second that you're going to take him home? Well that's him.

Only he took me home.

I'll take your bag, he said, and even though he's about half a mile shorter than me and has arms about as thick as a dog leg, he grabs my bag, and I grab it back and say Where's your mom, is she in the car?

And he smiles and takes a drag on his cigarette, which even though I know smoking kills and all that, I think is a little bit cool, but maybe all the kids in England smoke cigarettes? I don't say anything in case it's a well-known fact that the smoking age in England is something like twelve and by making a big thing about it I'll end up looking like an idiot when I've barely been here five minutes. Anyway, he says Mum couldn't come to the airport 'cause she's working and it's not worth anyone's life to interrupt her while she's working, and everyone else seemed to be somewhere else, so I drove here myself.

I looked at him funny then.

You drove here yourself? You DROVE HERE yourself? Yeah well and I'm the Duchess of Panama's Private Secretary.

And then he gave a little shrug and a little dog-shelter-dog kind of tilt of his head and he pointed at a falling-apart black jeep and he opened the door by reaching in through the window which was open, and pulling the handle up and yanking. He threw my bag in the back, though more like pushed it in, because it was pretty heavy, and then said Get in Cousin Daisy, and there was nothing else I could think of to do so I got in.

I'm still trying to get my head around all this when instead of following the signs that say Exit he turns the car up on to this grass and then drives across to a sign that says Do Not Enter and of course he Enters and then he jogs left across a ditch and suddenly we're out on the highway.

Can you believe they charge thirteen pounds fifty just to park there for an hour? he says to me.

Well to be fair, there is no way I'm believing any of this, being driven along on the wrong side of the road by this skinny kid dragging on a cigarette and let's face it who wouldn't be thinking what a weird place England is.

And then he looked at me again in his funny doggy way, and he said You'll get used to it. Which was strange too, because I hadn't said anything out loud.

Three

I fell asleep in the jeep because it was a long way to get to their house and watching the highway go by always makes me want to close my eyes. And then when I opened them again, there was this welcoming committee staring at me through the window and in it were four kids, and a goat and a couple of dogs who I later got told were called Jet and Gin, and in the background I saw some cats scooting around after a bunch of ducks that for some reason or other were hanging around on the lawn.

And for a minute I was so glad I was fifteen and from New York City because even though I haven't actually Seen It All, I have in fact seen more than plenty, and I have one of the best Oh Yeah, This Is So Much What I Usually Do kind of faces of anyone in my crowd. I put on that face right then, though let's be fair, all of this was taking me pretty much by surprise, because I didn't want them to think that kids from New York City are not at least as cool as English kids who just happen to live in huge ancient houses and have goats and dogs and all the rest.

There's still no Aunt Penn but Edmond introduces me to the rest of my cousins, who are called Isaac and Osbert and Piper, which I won't even begin to comment on. Isaac is Edmond's twin, and they look exactly the same, only Isaac's eyes are green and Edmond's are the same colour as the sky, which at the moment is grey. At first I liked Piper best because she just looked straight at me and said We are very glad you've come Elizabeth.

Daisy, I corrected her, and she nodded in a solemn kind of way that made me feel sure she'd remember.

Isaac started lugging my bag over to the house and then Osbert who's the oldest came and grabbed it away from him looking superior, and disappeared into the house with it.

Before I tell you what happened then, I have to tell you about the house, which is practically indescribable if the only sort of houses you've lived in before are apartments in New York City.

First let's get it clear that the house is practically falling down, but for some reason that doesn't seem to make any difference to how beautiful it is. It's made out of big chunks of yellowish stone, and has a steep roof, and is shaped like an L around a big courtyard with fat pebbles set in the ground. The short part of the L has a wide arched doorway and it used to be the stable, but now it's the kitchen and it's huge, with zigzag brick floors and big windows all across the front and a stable door that's left open Whenever it's not actually snowing, says Edmond.

Climbing up the front of the house is a huge vine with a stem so thick it must have been growing there for hundreds of years but there aren't any flowers on it yet, I guess because it's too early. Behind the house and up some stone steps is a square garden surrounded by high brick walls and in there are tons of flowers blooming already all in shades of white. In one corner there's a stone angel about the size of a child, very worn, with folded wings and Piper told me it was a child who lived in the house hundreds of years ago and is buried in the garden.

Later when I get a chance to look around the house I find out the inside is much more jumbled up than the outside with funny corridors that don't seem to lead anywhere and tiny bedrooms with slanty ceilings hidden away at the top of stairs. The stairs all creak and there are no curtains on any of the windows and all the main rooms seem huge after what I'm used to and they're scattered with big old comfortable furniture and paintings and books and huge fireplaces you can walk into and animals posing around the place to make it look even more authentic oldy-worldy.

The bathrooms turn out to be pretty oldy-worldy too or maybe I should say antique and make a huge noise whenever you want to do anything private.

Behind the house is tons of farmland some of which looks just like meadows and some of which is planted with potatoes and some is just starting to bloom in an acidy yellow colour which Edmond says is rape as in rapeseed oil but the only kind of rape I know is the kind you read about in the paper ten times a day and always ignore unless the rapist turns out to be a priest or someone on TV.

There's a farmer who comes and does all the planting because Aunt Penn always has Important Work To Do Related To The Peace Process and anyway wouldn't know the first thing about farming according to Edmond. But they keep sheep and goats and cats and dogs and chickens For Decoration said Osbert in a slightly sneery way and I'm getting the feeling about him that he's the one cousin who reminds me of people I knew in New York City.

Edmond and Piper and Isaac and Osbert, and Jet and Gin the black-and-white dogs, and a bunch of cats all went into the kitchen first and sat down at or under a wooden table and someone made cups of tea and then they all stared at me like I was something interesting they'd ordered from a zoo and asked me lots of questions in a much more polite way than would ever happen in New York, where kids would pretty much wait for some grown-up to come in all fake-cheerful and put cookies on a plate and make you say your names.

After a while I was feeling woozy and thought Boy, could I ever use a drink of freezing water to clear my head, and when I looked up Edmond was standing there holding one hand out and in it was a glass of water with ice cubes, and all the time looking at me with his almost-smiling look and though I didn't think much about this at the time, I noticed Isaac looking at Edmond in a funny way.

Then Osbert got up and left, he's sixteen and the oldest in case I didn't say it, which is a year older than me. Piper asked if I wanted to see the animals, or just lie down for a while, and I said lie down because even before I left New York I hadn't exactly been getting my fair share of sleep. She looked disappointed, but only for a second, and really I was feeling so much more tired than polite that I hardly cared.

She took me upstairs to a room down at the end of a hall which was the kind of room a monk would live in – smallish and plainish with thick white walls that weren't straight like new walls, and one huge window divided into lots of panes of yellowish and greenish glass. There was a big striped cat under the bed and some daffodils in an old bottle and suddenly that room seemed like the safest place I'd ever been in my life, which just goes to show how wrong a person can be about what's in store for them but here I go jumping the gun again.

We pushed my suitcase into a corner, and Piper came

in with a big pile of old blankets and she said in a shy way that they were woven from the sheep on the farm a long time ago and that the black ones were from the black sheep.

I pulled the black sheep blanket over my head and closed my eyes and for no good reason I could think of, I felt like I'd belonged to this house for centuries but that could have been wishful thinking.

And then I fell asleep.

Four

I didn't mean to sleep practically a whole day and a night but I did. And when I woke up I thought how strange it was to be lying in someone else's bed thousands of miles from home surrounded by greyish light and a weird kind of quiet that you never get in New York City where the traffic keeps you company in a constant buzzy way day and night.

The first thing I did was to check my phone for messages, but all it said was NO NETWORK and I thought Oh boy so much for civilization and felt a little freaked out and thought of that movie where they say No One Can Hear You Scream. But then I went over to the window and looked out and there was the slightest bit of pink light over to one side where the sun must have just started coming up and a totally quiet grey mist hung over the barn and the gardens and the fields, and everything was perfectly still and beautiful and I stared and stared expecting to see a deer or maybe a unicorn trotting home after a hard night but I didn't see anything except some birds.

After a while I was cold and got back under the blankets.

I felt too shy to come out of my room, so I stayed there and thought about my old home which unfortunately led to thinking about Davina the Diabolical, who sucked my father's soul out through his you-know-what and then got herself knocked up with the devil's spawn which, when it pops out, Leah and I are going to call Damian even if it's a girl.

According to my best friend Leah, D. the D. would have liked to poison me slowly till I turned black and swelled up like a pig and died in agony but I guess that plan flopped when I refused to eat anything and in the end she got me sent off to live with a bunch of cousins I'd never met a few thousand miles away while she and Dad and the devil's spawn went on their merry way. If she was making even the slightest attempt to address centuries of bad press for stepmothers, she scored a Big Fat Zero.

Before I could work myself up into a full-blown attack of hyperventilating, I heard a tiny noise at the door and there was Piper again, looking in, and when she saw I was awake she gave a little happy squeak like a mouse-cheer and asked Did I want a cup of tea?

OK, I said, and then Thank you, remembering to be polite, and I smiled at her because I still liked her from yesterday. And off she drifted just like the fog on little cat feet.

I went to the window again and looked out and saw the mist had cleared and everything was so green and then I put some clothes on and managed to find the kitchen after discovering some pretty amazing rooms by mistake, and Isaac and Edmond were there eating marmalade on toast and Piper was making my tea and seeming worried that I'd had to get out of bed to get it. In New York, nine-year-olds usually don't do this kind of thing, but wait for some grown-up to do it for them, so I was impressed by her intrepid attitude but also kind of wondering if good old Aunt Penn had died and no one could figure out a good way to tell me.

Mum was working all night, said Edmond, so she's gone to bed but she'll be up for lunch and then you'll see her.

Well that answered that, thank you Edmond.

While I drank my tea I could see Piper squirming around wanting to tell me something and she kept looking at Edmond and Isaac who just looked back and at last she said Please come to the barn Daisy. And the Please was more like a command than a request, and then she gave her brothers a look like I couldn't help it! And when I got up to go with her she did the nicest thing, which was to hold my hand and it made me want to hug her, especially since Being Nice to Daisy hadn't been anyone's favourite hobby lately.

In the barn, which smelled like animals but in a nice way, she showed me a tiny black-and-white goat with square eyes and little stubby horns and a bell round its neck on a red collar and said his name was Ding and he was her goat but I could have him if I wanted and then I did hug her because Piper and the sweet baby goat were exactly as nice as each other.

Then she showed me a bunch of sheep with long tangly coats and some chickens that lay blue eggs and she found one in the straw that was still warm and gave it to me and even though I didn't know what to do with an egg straight from a chicken's bottom I thought it was a nice thing to do.

I can't wait to tell Leah about this place.

After a while I was feeling pretty shivery and told Piper that I had to lie down for a little while and she frowned at me and said You need to eat something because you look too thin and I said Christ Piper don't you start it's only jet lag, and she looked hurt but Jesus, that old broken record is one I don't need to hear from people I hardly even know.

When I got up again there was soup and cheese and a huge loaf of bread in the kitchen and Aunt Penn was there and when she saw me she came right up and put her arms around me and then stood back and looked at my face and just said Elizabeth, like it was the end of a sentence, and then after a while, You look just like your mother, which was obviously a gross exaggeration since she was beautiful and I'm not. Aunt Penn has the same eyes as Piper, all serious and watching you, and when we sat down to lunch she didn't give me any soup or anything but just said Please Daisy, help yourself to whatever you'd like.

I told them all about Dad and Davina the Diabolical and Damian the devil's spawn and they laughed but you could tell they felt kind of sorry for me, and Aunt Penn said Well Their Loss Is Our Gain, which was nice even if she was just being polite.

I tried to study her without being too obvious because I was hoping to get some kind of clue from the way she looked and acted about the mother I barely ever got a chance to meet. She made a point to ask me lots of questions about my life and listened very carefully to the answers like she was trying to figure something out about me but not in the way most adults do, pretending to listen while thinking about some-thing else.

She asked how my father was and said she hadn't seen him in many years and I told her he was fine except for his taste in girlfriends which was totally un-fine, but he was probably feeling lots better now that I wasn't around reminding him about it day and night.

She smiled a funny kind of smile just then like she was trying to keep from laughing or maybe crying, and when I looked at her eyes I could see she was on my side which as far as I'm concerned made a nice change and I guess had something to do with my mother being her younger sister who died.

There was a fair amount of arguing and talking at lunch and except for talking to me she didn't get too involved but kind of observed, and overall I'd have to say that the main feeling you got from her was that she was a little distracted, I suppose because of the work she was doing.

A little later when all the others were talking she put her hand on my arm and said in a low voice just to me that she wished my mother were here to see how I'd turned into such a vivid person and I thought Vivid? That's a pretty strange word to choose, and I wondered if what she actually meant to say was Screwed Up. But then again maybe not because she didn't seem like the type to sit around thinking up ways to be bitchy, unlike some people I know.

After looking at me for a few seconds more she put her hand up very gently and pushed the hair off my face in a way that for some reason made me feel incredibly sad and then she said in a regretful grave voice that she was sorry but she had to give a lecture in Oslo at the end of the week on the Imminent Threat of War and had work to do so would I please excuse her? She would only be gone a few days in Oslo and the children would take good care of me. And I thought there's that old war again, popping up like a bad penny.

I didn't spend much time thinking about the war

because I was bored with everyone jabbering on for about the last five years about Would There Be One Or Wouldn't There and I happen to know there wasn't anything we could do about it anyway so why even bring the subject up.

It was when I was thinking things like this that I sometimes noticed Edmond looking at me in his odd, listening kind of way and sometimes I looked back at him doing the same expression myself just to see what he'd say. But mostly he just smiled and half closed his eyes and looked more like Wise Dog than ever and I thought to myself If this kid turns out to be thirty-five I won't be a bit surprised.

So that was pretty much all that happened on my first conscious day in England, and so far I was finding Life With My Cousins more than OK and a huge improvement over my so-called life at home on Eighty-sixth Street.

Late that night I heard the phone ring somewhere in the house and I wondered if it was my father calling to say Hey I made a mistake sending my only daughter away to another country because of some scheming harpy's ruthless whims, but by that time I was too sleepy to bother getting up and wandering around looking for a keyhole to listen at. So as you can see, that old country air must be doing me heaps of good already.

Five

Early the next morning I was strolling around as usual in my unpleasantly populated subconscious when I heard Edmond's voice very close to my ear saying Daisy Wake Up! And there was his face right near mine and a burning cigarette in one hand and some kind of striped Turkish slippers on his feet, and he said Come on we're going fishing.

And I forgot to say I hate fishing, and fish too now that you mention it, and instead pulled myself out from under my blankets and put on some clothes without washing or anything and next thing I knew Edmond and Isaac and Piper and I were sitting in the jeep and bumping down a bumpy old road and the sun was streaming in the windows and it felt much nicer than usual to be alive even if it meant a bunch of fish were going to have to die.

Edmond was driving with the rest of us crammed into the front seat and not wearing seat belts because there weren't any and Piper singing a song I'd never heard before with a funny jagged melody and her voice as pure as an angel.

We got to a place by a river and parked the jeep and got out and Isaac carried all the fishing stuff, and Edmond brought lunch and a blanket to lie on and although the day wasn't very warm, I made a nest for myself by trampling down a little patch in the tall grass and put the blanket down and lay very still and as the sun rose up in the sky I warmed up even more and all I could hear was the sound of Edmond talking in a steady low stream of conversation to the fish, and Piper singing her odd song, and the occasional splash of the river or a bird rising into the air near us and singing its heart out.

I was thinking about almost nothing except that bird and then Edmond was next to my ear whispering Skylark, and I just nodded, knowing it was futile to ask how he knew the answers to questions you hadn't even got around to asking yet. Then he handed me a hot cup of tea from the thermos and disappeared again back to the fishing.

No one caught much of anything, except Piper who caught a trout and threw it back (Piper always throws fish back, said Edmond, and Isaac said nothing as usual). It couldn't have been nicer as long as I didn't sit up because there was a coldish wind, so I lay there all dreamy and thought about Aunt Penn, and my life so far, and got a little bit of a flashback of what it was like to be happy.

It was times like this when I let my guard down for something like half a nanosecond, that Mom had a habit of strolling into my brain. Even though she was dead, which made people put on this sickening pious kind of face and say Oh I AM sorry, like it was their fault and in fact if everyone wasn't so busy apologizing all the time about asking a perfectly normal question like Where's your mother? I might have managed to get more information out of someone than just She Died To Give You Life, which is the party line on Good Old Mom.

It's a shame, starting out your first day on the planet as a murderer but there you go, I didn't have much choice at the time. Still, I could live quite happily without the labels I picked up because of it. Murderer or Poor Motherless Lamb.

Which one would you choose, the rock or the hard place?

Dad was one of those Never Mention Her Name Again type of fathers which if you ask me was extremely un-psychologically correct of him. Leah's father worked on Wall Street and shot himself one day when he lost six hundred million dollars of someone else's money and they never shut up about him in their house. Which, as Leah likes to point out, is not the perfect answer either.

I sometimes wished someone would just fill me in on the simple boring things like did she have big feet or wear make-up and what was her favourite song and did she like dogs or have a nice voice and what books did she read etc. I made up my mind to ask Aunt Penn some of these questions when she came back from Oslo but I guess what you really want to know arc the things you can't ask like Did she have eyes like yours and When you pushed my hair back was that what it feels like to have your mother do it and Did her hands look serious and quiet like yours and Did she ever have a chance to look at me with a complicated expression like the one on your face, and by the way Was she scared to die.

Then Edmond and Piper came and lay down on the blanket, one on either side of me with Piper holding my hand as usual and Isaac still standing in the water looking peaceful and they started arguing about what flies trout liked best in a quiet lazy sort of way, and Edmond blew smoke rings in the air and I closed my eyes and wished they were mine.

Six

I hardly saw Osbert that week because he went to school, unlike Isaac and Edmond and Piper, who were supposed to be Home Schooled, which as far as I could tell meant reading whatever books you happen to be interested in, and every once in a blue moon having Aunt Penn say Have you learned any geography? and them saying yes.

Now this was clearly one of the greatest improvements on the education system since time began and I was greatly looking forward to being enrolled but Aunt Penn said that I didn't have to do much of anything until autumn term, which didn't start until September, and by that time no one was going to school anyway due to the You Know What.

Without anyone making a big deal of it or punching me on the shoulder and saying You're OK Cousin Daisy like they do on TV, Piper and Edmond and Isaac and I started doing pretty much everything together, though sometimes I forgot to count Isaac because he could go days without saying a single word. I knew Aunt Penn wasn't worried about him because I heard her say to someone that he'd speak when he was ready to speak, but all I could think was in New York that kid would have been stuck in a straitjacket practically from birth and dangled over a tank full of Educational Consultants and Remedial Experts all snapping at his ankles for the next twenty years arguing about his Special Needs and getting paid plenty for it.

I went quietly down to Aunt Penn's office a few nights later hoping I might be able to send some e-mails to all the people who must have thought I'd disappeared off the face of the earth and there was a light under the door and Aunt Penn's voice said Edmond? I thought at first I'd say nothing, just creep away, but at the last minute I changed my mind and said No, it's Daisy. Aunt Penn said Oh Daisy please come in, and she looked so happy to see me and said Sit by the fire a minute. Even though it was April it was freezing cold at night and she said You wouldn't believe what it costs to heat this draughty old house.

I huddled up close to the fire and she put her work away saying she'd done more than enough for one night and when she saw I was still shivering she got up from her chair and wrapped a blanket around me, all the time with a look on her face like a smile only sadder and then she sat down next to me on the sofa and started telling me about her sister and it took me a second to realize the person she meant was my mother.

She told me things I never knew like how my mother was all set to go to university to study history when she fell in love with my father and decided not to go after all, which made their father furious. When she went away to live in America hardly any of the family was speaking to her. Then from the top of her desk Aunt Penn took down a framed picture of two young women looking almost the same, one of them laughing and one looking serious and holding on to the neck of a huge wild-looking grey dog Aunt Penn said was called Lady, As a joke, because she had no manners at all, but look how your mother adored her.

I've seen plenty of pictures of my mother at home, but almost always with my father and not a single one taken before he knew her, so this was strange because she looked so different, happy and young like someone you've known in another life. Aunt Penn said I could keep the photograph but I said No thank you because it seemed to belong to that desk and that room, and I didn't want to drag it away to a foreign place.

Aunt Penn rubbed one hand across her eyes and said it was late and we both needed to go to bed but just as I was getting to the door she said When your mother phoned to tell me she was pregnant, she sounded happier than she'd ever sounded in her whole life about that baby. Which was you, Daisy. Then she told me to run upstairs before I caught cold but it seemed like hours before I stopped shivering.

The next day Aunt Penn set off for Oslo and we didn't think much about it except that we were In Charge and pretty happy about it, but later when you look back on the whole story you realize that the moment she left was exactly the moment we all started skewing off into crisis like how Archduke Ferdinand getting killed started WWI even though the connection, to me at least, was never that clear.

At the time she just kissed each of us and smiled and told us to be sensible and there was something about the way she didn't even miss a beat when it came to kissing me that made me feel better than almost all the nice things that had happened since I arrived.

We didn't get much of a chance to sit back and enjoy being orphans before things started happening.

The first thing that happened wasn't our fault. That was a bomb that went off in the middle of a big train station in London the day after Aunt P went to Oslo and something like seven or seventy thousand people got killed.

This obviously went down very badly with the populace at large and was pretty scary etc. but to be honest it didn't seem to have that much to do with us way off in the country. How it did affect us was it made them close all the airports, which meant no one could get home for the foreseeable future, namely Aunt Penn.

None of us quite dared say that having no parents at all was pretty cool, but you didn't have to be a mind-reader to figure it out. Basically we couldn't believe our luck, and for a little while it felt like we were on some big train rolling down a hill, and all we cared about was how great it felt to be going fast.

That same day after the first bomb went off everyone just sat glued to the television and the radio, and the telephone kept ringing asking us if we were OK, but given we were about four million miles from the epicentre I'd say we stood a pretty good chance of surviving.

Of course everyone was talking about food shortages and shutting down transport and calling up all the able-bodied men and basically all the Gloom and Doom stuff they could possibly think up in the limited time allotted, and the guys on the radio were talking in solemn voices asking anyone they could drag off the street Whether This Meant War and then we had to listen to all the solemn experts pretending to have the inside track when any one of them would have given his left arm to know the game plan himself.

Eventually my father got through from the office and I guess hearing my voice convinced him I was still alive and there was nothing to worry about because afterwards we had our usual conversation, him saying How are you do you need any money or want to come home and me just answering Yes yes no no whatever.

He said they were all worried about me but I couldn't think who THEY might be and then he said he had a meeting so he had to go but he loved me and when I didn't say anything he hung up.

Well I couldn't take much more of all the blah blah blah so Edmond and I walked down the long hill to the village which was extremely picturesque and full of little houses all connected up and made out of the same yellowy stone as our house. It wasn't very big but there were lots of little roads with identical houses, except for different knick-knacks in the windows, spreading out on either side of the main street and Edmond said it was big enough to have a weekly market and three bakeries, two butchers, a church originally from the twelfth century, a tea shop, two pubs (one good, one bad, the bad one with a hotel), a number of lifelong drunks, at least one suspected child molester, and a shoe store that also sold raincoats and waterproof boots and footballs and penny candy and Tweety Bird backpacks.

There was one building near the centre that was a little bigger and squarer than all the rest and that was the town hall and across from it was a cobbled square where the market appeared every Wednesday and in one corner diagonally opposite was one of the pubs. It was named The Salmon because of the fishmonger next door but when the fishmonger shut down no one bothered to change the name. In the other corner was a

Ye Olde English version of a 7-Eleven, which for some reason was also a post office and a drugstore and sold newspapers out front if all else failed.

We went in, and with the money Aunt Penn had left for the weekend bought as much bottled water and canned things as we could carry home which was a lot more fun than staring at the same old picture of Smoking Carnage on TV and we tried to be very mature about the kind of food we might need in a siege, which let's face it, wasn't the most likely scenario for the back of beyond. We weren't the only ones at the shop, but people were fairly friendly especially to two kids on their own and no one tried to kick us to the ground and steal our pear halves.

That still left a whole afternoon with the end of the world about to happen, so we walked back up the hill to the house, more slowly this time because of all the bottled water, and when we got there Edmond decided we should move up and camp at the lambing barn because it was over a mile away from the house and so well hidden behind a group of big oak trees that no one would find it if they didn't know what they were looking for. We figured if The Enemy was going to come all the way down here, we'd better think of a way to make ourselves totally invisible, though in fact the main reason was that it was something to do.

So Piper and Isaac and Edmond and I started dragging provisions and blankets and books up to the lambing barn, which usually just stored hay, and except for the mice it was comfortable and dry and had water for when it was used for lambing, so we told Osbert we were staying up there for the foreseeable future, but he barely seemed to notice because he was busy watching nothing happening on the news and calling his friends and looking worried trying to figure out along with sixty million other people whether we were In A War Or Not.

Anyway, it was around mid-afternoon that we settled in and Piper brought Osbert's *Boy Scout Survival Handbook* and decided that we had to collect and cook all our own food, so she hiked all the way back to the house and gathered some blue eggs and dug up some early potatoes from the next field over and threatened to dry worms on a stone and grind them into powder to add protein to stews. As none of us was short of protein except me and I was used to it, we managed to convince her to save the worm powder for a rainy day and she looked a little crestfallen but didn't press the point.

While she was foraging for food Isaac arrived from the house with a big straw bag full of cheese and ham and a fruitcake in a tin and dried apricots and a big bottle of apple juice and a thick slab of plain chocolate wrapped in brown paper.

We hid the bag in a feedbox so we wouldn't hurt Piper's feelings and what she served in the end wasn't exactly a meal fit for a king, but it had the right feel for an emergency. Edmond and Isaac made a fire and baked the potatoes right in it, and then when it died down Piper put the eggs in the coals on the side and though some turned out sort of raw on the side that wasn't towards the fire, they apparently tasted OK.

I told them I was too excited to eat anything, and that seemed fine with everyone except Edmond who looked at me in his way as usual and I noticed that once you realize someone's watching you it's pretty hard not to find yourself watching them back.

Afterwards we made up one big bed in the hay loft by spreading blankets down and we took our shoes off and got in together, still in our clothes, first Isaac, then Edmond, then me and then Piper in that order and though we kept a decent distance at first, eventually we just gave up and moved together because of the bats flying all around, and the sounds of the crickets which can be very lonely, and the cold night and the thought of all those dead people a million miles away in London. I wasn't used to sleeping that close to anyone else and much as I liked having Piper always holding on to my hand it kind of restricted how much I could turn over and I'm pretty sure I was the last one to fall asleep.

I could hear Jet and Gin down below us in the barn, and a long time after I thought he was asleep Edmond said in a quiet voice that the dogs always stayed up here during lambing because that's when they were needed most for rounding up the sheep and we were probably confusing them by being here now. And the soft sound of his voice made me want to move closer to him so I did, a little, and for a while we just looked at each other without blinking or saying a word. Then he moved his head to the right just enough so he could brush his cheek against the part of my arm that was near his face and after that he closed his eyes and fell asleep while I lay there and wondered if that's the feeling you're supposed to have when your cousin touches a totally innocent part of your anatomy that's even fully clothed.

I lay there for a while more, smelling the smell of tobacco in Edmond's hair and waiting to fall asleep, and I remembered thinking about a painting we had to copy in art class once called *The Calm Before The Storm*. It showed an old-fashioned sailing ship on a dead flat sea and the sky behind it was all sorts of gold and orange and red colours and it looked like the picture of peace if you hadn't noticed the greenish-black section up in one corner, which was obviously The Storm. For some reason I used to think about that painting a lot, I guess because of that feeling you get when you know that something awful is going to happen and no one in the painting does and if you could only warn them then the rest of their lives might be different.

The Calm Before The Storm seemed like the right sort of phrase to jump into a person's mind on this occasion no matter how happy I was just at the moment because given how my life had gone so far, I'd had lots of practice in not expecting everything to turn out like your basic Hollywood tear jerker with the blind girl played by this year's Oscar Hopeful and the crippled boy miraculously walking and everyone going home happy.

Seven

The next day, without actually saying that we were abandoning our plan to live in the barn, we kind of gravitated back towards the house to have a bath and get clean clothes because if you want to know the truth about how romantic it is to sleep in a barn, it isn't very, due to the hay itching and the bats and how cold it gets at night even though it's supposed to be spring.

Back at the house Osbert was annoyed because he'd had to milk the goats himself and it was Piper's job, and it turned out that Aunt Penn had called from Oslo and told him she was doing everything in her power to get home and in the meantime there was some money in the bank account to tide us over, and she'd already spoken to the bank manager about us getting it. Osbert said she sounded more worried about the world than about us, but he didn't seem annoyed at being second best and Piper said It's because she knows we'll be fine.

For a second while Osbert was talking about Aunt

Penn, Edmond's face looked very pale, but he was facing Isaac so I couldn't be absolutely sure and when he turned around again he looked fairly normal and said There are people all over the world who will help her if they can. And that was the end of the conversation.

The good old Royal Mail didn't seem to have any clue that there was a war starting up and that day there was a letter from my dad, and one from Leah. Dad yammered on a lot about Davina the D. and how she was feeling what with the pregnancy and all, like it was preying on my mind that she might be feeling uncomfortable when in fact I just hoped her ankles would swell up like balloons and her breasts would sag down to her knees and the silicone in them turn to cement. There was a little something stuck on at the end of the letter about missing me, and how I should be careful not to become a Victim Of The Terrorist Threat and had I managed to gain any weight blah blah blah.

Leah's letter was much more entertaining, with reports that Ms Cool Herself, Melissa Banner, was going around telling everyone that she and Lyle Hershberg were Hooking Up. Well if this banner headline is true, I swear to god I will assign all my worldly goods to the Salvation Army and I'd say there's no danger of some religious tuba player ending up with my DVD player given that Lyle was famous for telling his last girlfriend Mimi Maloney that if she didn't Satisfy His Needs at least three times a day he'd have to find Relief elsewhere and Melissa Banner is the world's most famous living professional virgin. Leah walked in once on Lyle Satisfying His Needs all by himself in homeroom when everyone should have been at school assembly and she said Well well well Lyle Hershberg, don't look now but there's a Smurf with a hard-on in your pants. Or at least she claims that's what she said but not to be disloyal or anything I've always had my doubts.

I wanted to talk all this through with Leah right then and there and I nearly cried with how much I missed having a cell phone that worked and e-mail even if I did have a hundred and twelve wacky cousins instead.

So I sat down and wrote back all about Edmond and Piper and Isaac and the animals and the house and the war, and I made it sound even better than it actually was, and by the time I finished the letter I'd convinced myself that This Was The Life oh yes and Boy Had I Lucked Out. But it's easier said than done to convince yourself that god has smiled on you when the actual fact is that you're living with strangers due to the evil workings of your wicked stepmother not to mention your official next of kin.

Then in came Osbert again with a face like a dead pigeon and said there were more attacks this time in the USA.

And when, to seem interested, I said How terrible, where? He said Pittsburgh and Detroit and Houston only he pronounced it Hoos-ton. Well part of me was fairly pleased they hadn't bombed the Upper West Side and part of me started having this pretty good fantasy about Dad and Davina all bandaged up and limping and trying to come live here with us and us saying We are just SO SORRY but the airports are shut otherwise we'd simply LOVE to have you, really we would.

I tried eating a little bit of bacon today because Edmond particularly asked me to but it tasted like pig and I gagged.

Eight

I'm thinking now would be a good time to talk about Isaac because he's the one who gets left out of most of the action due to hardly ever saying a word but I'm starting to realize it's the ones who aren't yakking all the time who sometimes turn out to be worth keeping an eye on.

At first I barely noticed him what with noticing Edmond so much and Piper holding my hand all the time and chickens clucking, dogs barking, sheep baaing, not to mention half the world blowing up and the pipes banging night and day. So it took me longer than usual to get the picture that while Piper and Edmond were busy watching over me, Isaac was busy watching over them.

He didn't do it in an obvious way like Osbert who was always pushing himself into the conversation with superior information and making it clear that he was the one with Family Responsibilities which Frankly Exhausted Him and He'd Rather Not Be Bothered only

Seeing As How He Was The Eldest, Well, deep sigh.

Edmond on the other hand was totally upfront even if he did surprise you in about half a million ways each day. When Edmond was listening in to your thoughts, you could tell by looking at him looking at you.

Isaac was more shadowy and Kept His Counsel. This doesn't mean there was anything sneaky about his way of watching, or anything sentimental either. He just accepted the things people did, without comment or judgement and maybe without being terribly concerned. Even his family seemed to interest him in an abstract way, like lab specimens he'd come to feel responsibility and affection for.

At times I thought he was more animal than human. For instance if you were walking in town on market day and there were tons of people milling around, you would never have to worry about losing him in the crowd even if you totally forgot he was there and got separated for ages. You could zig and zag and make turns on a sudden whim and stop for tea and cut across a few back streets and decide that today would be a good time to do something totally different and try that bakery that none of you normally went to when in actual fact you had plenty of bread already at home so there'd be no reason to be in a bakery at all, and the next time you looked up Isaac would be right at your elbow, totally casual, like he'd been there all along or possibly just followed your train of thought through the crowd.

It was like he understood humans objectively and could see your entire life stretching out in both directions including whether you were going to make a detour to the bakery and which one and when.

With non-humans he was completely different. With a dog or horse or badger or fox every fibre of his being was totally engaged. Even his face was different around animals, with the expression of polite distance he always wore for humans replaced by something concentrated and alive.

They knew it too. You could search hours for a pregnant cat and Isaac would tell you to look under the hessian in the garden shed and there she'd be with five kittens, probably already having told him what each one was named. Piper said people used to borrow him when they went to buy a new dog because he could always see if something wasn't quite right just by looking, or if it was the type to savage your new baby to death on a whim.

You might wonder, as I did, what a dog or a sheep had to say to a person like Isaac that's so interesting but I guess he might have said the same thing about a foreign life form like me. What have I ever said that's so riveting to anyone but myself?

Shrinks don't count. They listen for cash.

Nine

Today there was a knock on the door and it turned out to be two bored-looking men From The Council coming to register us and Determine Our Medical And Nutritional Exigencies which turned out to mean did any of us have appendicitis or scurvy?

They had a list about as thick as a phone book with names and addresses and some were checked off and some crossed out and there were hundreds of question marks scattered around the pages and boy did you ever get the sense that they wished they'd asked a few more questions before signing up for this job.

After finding Aunt Penn on the list and putting a bunch of Xs and a question mark by her name and asking a few official-type questions, they asked to speak to our guardian and seemed fairly taken aback to discover that the closest we had to a grown-up on the premises was Osbert.

But seeing as how there wasn't much they could do about our situation short of filing an official report that no one would ever notice or read or care about, they decided to stick to the questions they'd asked everyone else for miles around like, Were any of the animals on the farm kept for food? Osbert said the sheep were very rare and kept for breeding and wool and for selling on to other farms, and the goats were pets but the hens were all layers which struck me as funny because after that all I could think of was layers and layers of hens.

Then they asked for everyone's names and ages and Osbert said that I was their American cousin and they looked even more confused and wanted to see my passport and then asked lots of questions about Dad and what was he doing sending his only daughter away from home at a time like this and I said Well don't think that question hasn't occurred to me too.

Then they both looked at me with the evil eye I seem to get from just about everyone these days and asked if we had enough money for food, and Osbert explained that we had some money in his mother's account and the men said, We'll do what we can for you, and added that it wasn't definite but rationing would probably start any day now due to the embargoes, and school was closing early for summer holidays and we should stay off the roads. Like hanging around on the roads was the world's best entertainment.

We asked them what was going to happen next and how long they thought the war would last but by the totally blank looks they gave us in return you got the sense that none of these questions had occurred to them before.

Well it was reassuring to know that local government was taking an interest, but their visit didn't exactly cause any radical changes to our lifestyle since for the last few days we'd mostly been hanging around wondering what to do next, broken up by trips to town where we had to wait in line for hours listening to people gossip about what was Really Going On. The short answer if you ask me was that nobody had the slightest clue but it sure didn't stop them pretending they did.

People who had friends or friends of friends who had managed to get phone calls or e-mails through said that London Was Occupied and there were tanks and soldiers in the streets and fire and anarchy all around. Supposedly the hospitals were filled to bursting with all the people who'd been poisoned or bombed and everyone was fighting over food and drinkable water.

One crazy old man kept whispering to anyone who would listen that the BBC had been taken over by Malign Forces and that we shouldn't believe anything we heard on The Wireless but his wife rolled her eyes and said he was still worried about the Germans from last time around.

I saw expressions on people's faces that I'd never seen before, something like anxiety and superiority and paranoia all mixed up in one polite grimace. Everyone tried to look like they knew all about all the news already, or that they had Much More Recent Information but weren't At Liberty to give it away.

Each day we'd walk down the hill to the village and hang around in a line outside the village shop waiting for our turn to get inside and choose a few essentials. For some reason it reminded me of *Supermarket Sweep* which I'd always wanted to go on, only there wasn't much in the way of food and you weren't allowed to run around stuffing as much as possible into bags.

The worst part was having to listen to everyone's crackpot theories and there was no hope you could pretend to be deaf due to it being such a small town and everybody knowing everything about you.

Here's the sort of thing we'd hear, all in low hushed tones especially when us Children were around, and if it doesn't sound so bad to you try playing it on an endless loop while you listen and smile politely until your cheeks go into spasm and you develop a twitch:

1. My brother-in-law says it's the French bastards.
2. My friend in Chelsea said the looting is terrible and she got the most amazing wide-screen TV.
3. My neighbour in The Lords says it's the Chinese.
4. Have you noticed that no Jews have been killed?

5. There's a nuclear bunker under Marks & Spencer that's only open to shareholders.
6. People are eating their pets.
7. The Queen is Bearing Up.
8. The Queen is Breaking Down.
9. The Queen is one of Them.

You can imagine it was the social event of the day, everyone competing for the worst piece of news.

One of the couples who lived in London but had a weekend house near the village was here for The Duration, saying that they had two kids and a pure-bred Bouvier des Flandres, which turns out to be a dog, and they figured it would be a whole lot safer here than in London. Well they were probably right about it being safer if you didn't count the locals who were suddenly getting all Them and Us all over the place. So far it was fairly civilized but you could see that under the surface everyone hated those people and their fancy French-sounding dog and were just waiting for a chance to get even when the food ran out.

A lot of worried families asked if we needed a place to stay because of Aunt Penn being gone but it was obvious they didn't really want us even if we'd wanted them, which we didn't. Sometimes when we said No thank you, they looked so relieved we couldn't help feeling a little hurt.

As every day passed you could see the panic on more

and more people's faces, and the rest carefully composed their features to look sombre and made clucking noises and said How Awful It Was. But once we were away from them we actually felt pretty cheerful and laughed on the walk back to the house, partly to cheer Piper up and partly because it still felt like an adventure and because the sun was shining and it was a beautiful walk, war or no war.

I was desperate to tell Leah about all this stuff and how totally great it was to have no grown-ups around telling you what to do all the time. Not that I went around saying that out loud, but let's face it. No matter how much you put on a sad expression and talked about how awful it was that all those people were killed and what about Democracy and the Future Of Our Great Nation the fact that none of us kids said out loud was that WE DIDN'T REALLY CARE. Most of the people who got killed were either old like our parents so they'd had good lives already, or people who worked in banks and were pretty boring anyway, or other people we didn't know.

Osbert and his friends from school said they thought it would be amazing to live in London and be spies and duck around The Enemy trying to get information and I thought, right, Osbert and a bunch of his snotty schoolboy friends would be the first people I'd fall back on to save the nation if I happened to be Prime Minister.

One afternoon I found Edmond in the lower barn

feeding the animals and I played with Ding while he milked the goats. Ding was as nice as a puppy and would just butt you politely with his head until you rubbed his ears and then he'd stand there in a kind of trance with his eyes closed leaning on you more and more the more you rubbed and if you stepped away he'd fall over.

After a while we took the milk back to the house and it started to rain and Edmond and I went and sat in my room and he smoked and we talked about lots of things and he asked me all sorts of questions that usually drive me insane like why I didn't eat much.

For some reason I didn't get mad at him for asking, and I really tried to explain about at first not wanting to get poisoned by my stepmother and how much it annoyed her and how after a while I discovered I liked the feeling of being hungry and the fact that it drove everyone stark raving mad and cost my father a fortune in shrinks and also it was something I was good at.

He didn't look at me while I was talking, but after a few minutes he lay back and let his knee rest against my knee and I got another one of those feelings you're not supposed to get from your cousin and I wondered very quietly to myself What Was Happening Here but of course it doesn't matter how quietly you wonder things when Edmond is listening. It takes a whole lot of practice to get used to being careful about what you think in the privacy of your own brain. On the other hand, there are advantages in being able to think something that you can count on being overheard. It eliminates a fair bit of fumbling around.

Do you ever think about dying? Edmond asked me, talking on a tangent.

And I said Yes all the time but mostly as a way of making other people feel guilty.

And he didn't say anything but when, a lot later, I went over the conversation in my head I realized I never asked him the same question back.

We were quiet for the longest time just listening to the rain on the window with his leg resting against mine and a feeling flying between us in a crazy jagged way like a bird caught in a room. The feeling which had been starting up for a while now was so strong it made me dizzy and so far we'd just been pretending it was what cousinly love felt like and all that garbage you tell yourself when you want to pretend something's not really happening.

After some more time I tried an experiment by thinking something very very quietly to myself, and then nothing happened for ages. Edmond just lay there with his eyes closed and I felt a little disappointed and a little relieved all at the same time and then just as I was moving on to other things in my head, he propped himself up on one elbow and looked at me with a little half-smile and then kissed me on the mouth so gently and sweetly, and then we kissed again, only not quite so sweetly.

And after a little while of this my brain and my body and every single inch of me that was alive was flooded with the feeling that I was starving, starving, starving for Edmond.

And what a coincidence, that was the feeling I loved best in the world.

Ten

It would be much easier to tell this story if it were all about a chaste and perfect love between Two Children Against The World At An Extreme Time In History but let's face it that would be a load of crap.

The real truth is that the war didn't have much to do with it except that it provided a perfect limbo in which two people who were too young and too related could start kissing without anything or anyone making us stop. There were no parents, no teachers, no schedules. There was nowhere to go and nothing to do that would remind us that this sort of thing didn't happen in the Real World. There no longer *was* any Real World.

For a while Edmond and I pretended that what was happening between us was totally reversible. We drifted around through the day not looking at each other and acting like nothing at all had happened.

But it didn't matter. It turns out to be true that an Object In Motion Remains In Motion. Well thank you Miss Valerie Greene, science teacher back at dear old Nightingale-Bamford School For Girls. Whoever imagined anything you said would ever come in handy?

Now let's try to understand that falling into sexual and emotional thrall with an under-age blood relative hadn't exactly been on my list of Things To Do while visiting England, but I was coming around to the belief that whether you liked it or not, Things Happen and once they start happening you pretty much just have to hold on for dear life and see where they drop you when they stop.

In our case, Things Happened in spades.

The next thing that happened was we started sleeping most of the daylight hours so we could be awake at night when everyone else was in bed. Of course if you had to choose an audience for illicit love based on the people you'd least like to have hanging around, Piper and Isaac would win hands down. Isaac because he always knew by a sort of navigational instinct where Edmond was and what he was thinking, in case it wasn't totally obvious anyway just by looking at us. And Piper because she was so good and pure that when she was confused about what was going on she just stood and stared at your face until you either told her the truth or ran away and hid. Neither of us was anxious to tell her the truth so most of the time we hid.

Things were so intense I was sure that other people could hear the hum coming off us. Piper and Isaac didn't say anything but the dogs were upset and behaved strangely, as if the hum and the smell of our skin made them anxious. Gin refused to leave Edmond's side, wrapping herself round his legs when he tried to go anywhere, and crawling up into his armpit whenever he sat down as if she wanted to hide herself inside him. It got so bad that he had to be stroking her all the time or she'd start whining piteously until Osbert shouted from the other room Will someone make that dog shut up!

Some nights Edmond had to lock her in the barn if we wanted to be alone but secretly I felt desperate for her because I knew exactly how she felt.

Osbert was the only one who didn't seem suspicious. He was so interested in the Decline of Western Civilization that he missed the version of it taking place under his nose.

We didn't hear anything from Aunt Penn. It had been a few weeks since she left and every moment of every day felt like some bizarre new existence in which Not Hearing From Aunt Penn fit perfectly. You could tell Piper missed her mother and there were things I still wanted to ask her but aside from that her arrival right now in the middle of the world's most inappropriate case of sexual obsession would have been inconvenient to say the least.

As for me? I was pretty far gone, but not so far gone that I thought anyone with half a toehold in reality would think what we were doing was a good idea.

But I would like to make an important point before this goes any further and that is if anyone feels like arresting me for corrupting an innocent kid then all I can say is that Edmond was *not corruptible*. Some people are just like that and if you don't believe me it just means you've never met one of them yourself.

Which is your loss.

Eleven

It was now five weeks since the war started.

Pretty much every day we heard about more bombs. The airports stayed closed and occasionally the electricity would sputter and go off. All the usual sources of information including e-mail and cell phones were much too slow and unreliable to be of any use and there was no television to speak of. According to Osbert you could try to send e-mails but they'd bounce back at you for no particular reason and the same with text messages. And sometimes they'd arrive, but not in the form you'd sent them. And sometimes you couldn't get anything like a dial tone for hours at a time and in the end it was easier just to give up and read a book.

None of this bothered me overmuch since no one ever tried to call me but I guess it made Osbert nervous because it was getting harder and harder to stay in touch with his spy-crazy friends who spent their lives organizing illicit jaunts down to the pub for exchanges of information. Though they practised looking grim, in fact they couldn't have been happier waiting for the real action to get going so they could smoke out collaborators and look danger in the eye while carrying messages across enemy lines.

We've all seen the movies.

Then just when we got used to our new life and our daily walk to town and waiting hours for a couple of loaves of bread and half a pound of butter and four pints of milk (because we're children) the whole countryside was quarantined due to an outbreak of smallpox or should I say an Alleged Outbreak Of Smallpox because these days we didn't know what was true and what wasn't, and Osbert and the food queue were virtually our only sources of information since even the voices on the radio sounded strange and when you could manage to tune in to them you didn't know who they were or whether they were telling you the truth, and there were no newspapers and the phone lines were dead more often than not.

Anyhow, the upshot of the so-called Smallpox Epidemic was that you weren't supposed to be out on the streets at all and now big black trucks went around and left bags of food twice a week at the end of the drive, and if you had any special requests you could write them on a piece of paper.

We thought this was pretty funny for a while, and wrote things like chocolate and sausages and cake and Coca-Cola on our list and then Piper got mad at us because she was the one who did most of the cooking and there were things she really needed, and all our stupid requests were getting in the way of them noticing that what we really needed was flour. Not that they paid any attention to our list anyway. We got what we got.

So OK there was smallpox. But because everything was getting worse by little daily increments and you didn't know what was true or not true it seemed easier just to treat this news as another fact of life and nothing particularly to worry about.

Think about it. It's May in the middle of the English Countryside. And everyone's saying It's the most beautiful May we've had in years and Isn't it ironic? From my point of view this made any doomsday scenario even harder to get my head around, especially having grown up in the Concrete Jungle, which possibly overstates the case given that the Upper West Side is fairly leafy, as concrete jungles go. But we're still talking about a few nice trees here and there whereas in England I was drowning in fertility. And although there were tons of rumours coming from every direction, nothing THAT BAD seemed to be happening to any of US.

Meanwhile about a hundred thousand white roses all over the front of the house are blooming like mad, the vegetables are growing about six inches a day, and the flower gardens all around the house are so full of colour that you couldn't help feeling ecstatic and dizzy just looking at them. According to one of Isaac's rare speeches, the birds were happier with the invasion than they'd been in years since no one was driving cars or farming or doing anything much to disturb them, so all they did was lay eggs and sing and try to avoid getting eaten by foxes.

It was getting to be like Walt Disney on E outside the house what with squirrels and hedgehogs and deer wandering around with the ducks and dogs and chickens and goats and sheep and if anyone looked totally disoriented by this whole war thing it was them.

Piper and Edmond and Isaac and I used to watch this lunatic fringe milling around every day at sunset and then Edmond and I would slip away to the tiny bedroom at the top of the house or the big storage closet under the eaves or the lambing barn or one of about a thousand places we'd found where we could try and try and try to get enough of each other but it was like some witch's curse where the more we tried to stop being hungry the more starving we got.

It was the first time in as long as I could remember that hunger wasn't a punishment or a crime or a weapon or a mode of self-destruction.

It was simply a way of being in love.

Sometimes I thought hours had passed when really it was minutes. Sometimes we fell asleep and then woke up to finish where we'd left off. Sometimes I felt like

I was being consumed from within like a person with one of those freak diseases where you digest your own stomach. And sometimes we had to stop, just because we were raw and exhausted and still humming humming humming with something we didn't even have the strength left to do anything about.

Then we would sleep for a little while and eventually reappear and try to act normal which meant things like helping Piper search for honeycomb or dandelion leaves or spending a few hours weeding the vegetable garden. All the sunshine meant there were vegetables earlier than there should have been, and given the dire straits we were supposedly in, there seemed to be lots of food. And of course being me, now that there was a war on and rationing and all, I was in deprivation heaven and hardly needed my father screwing Davina in the next room to help me lose my appetite for a few years.

The rest of them ate eggs and goat's milk and greens from the garden, and there were baked beans that we'd stockpiled and Piper was getting incredibly good at making things with the dried beans and rice and bacon they put in our package most weeks. There were starting to be tomatoes from the garden, and there were lots of beans and everyone except me missed bread which was getting harder to come by and especially Anchor butter which Edmond said he dreamed about though we made something I thought worked pretty well by beating the goat's milk for ages with a whisk.

One of the stranger things that we just came to accept was that no one seemed to know exactly where the food was coming from. At first they thought it must be the local council, but some people whispered that it was the Red Cross, or the Americans, and others suspected The Enemy, and lots of people wouldn't touch it at all Just In Case.

I was pretty happy to starve rather than eat food Davina made in peacetime but I never thought anyone was trying to poison us during the war. I tried eating a little more so Edmond would stop looking at me that way and after a week or so he even said I looked better by which I'm sure he meant fatter so I cut back some after that.

But I was talking about the quarantine.

According to what Osbert picked up in one of his clandestine spy-boy meetings down at the pub, the Smallpox Epidemic was just a rumour spread around to keep us all quiet and scared and out of the way.

Then we heard that people were dying.

Edmond said that it was measles not smallpox and that most people weren't dying, but because it was almost impossible to get antibiotics, people were dying of pretty ordinary stuff like pneumonia and bad cases of chickenpox, and broken bones and some women died having babies.

We got flyers in with our food saying to boil all our water and *Be Extra Careful When Handling Knives,*

Tools Or Firearms Because Minor Injuries Could Lead To Infection And Death. Which struck me as extremely amusing given that we're supposedly in the middle of a war, which usually has the same effect.

I didn't know if the food was poisoned. I didn't know whether we'd get an infection and die. I didn't know if a bomb would fall on us. I didn't know whether Osbert would expose us to spores from some deadly disease picked up during his secret meetings. I didn't know if we would be taken prisoner, tortured, murdered, raped, forced to confess or inform on our friends.

The only thing I knew for certain was that all around me was more life than I'd ever experienced in all the years I'd been on earth and as long as no one shut me in the barn away from Edmond at night I was safe.

Twelve

So there we are carrying on our happy little life of under-age sex, child labour and espionage when someone came to visit us which, after weeks of Just Us Five kind of took us by surprise, to put it mildly.

He was a not-too-bad-looking man of around thirty-five who seemed too tired even to pretend to be all polite and friendly and he said I'm sorry to bother you but have you got any drugs?

We all stood there and gaped at him and speaking personally I was wondering whether he was setting up some kind of small business venture to sell cocaine to people who were housebound, deprived of television and generally bored senseless by the war.

We must have looked pretty moronic just staring at him with our mouths open because he said Perhaps I should speak to your mother or father and then Osbert puffed himself up like he was going to make a big speech and said There's only us. So I guess he decided against the speech after all.

Then the guy looked puzzled and Osbert explained about Aunt Penn and even though he didn't say anything more, by the look on his face I was going to be surprised if that was the end of it as far as he was concerned even with all the other things he had to think about.

Then he picked up more or less where he left off and said I'm sorry, perhaps I should explain about the drugs, I'm Dr Jameson and as you've probably noticed there's a war on and we're trying to take care of the people in this area.

We didn't say anything and so he just kept talking.

The surgeries have all been shut down. The hospitals are on skeleton staff and trying to deal with casualties coming in from the cities and have confiscated most of the supplies from the chemists so local people with basic problems like high blood pressure or diabetes are experiencing difficulties. We're trying to keep these problems from becoming life-threatening, but what we need is medicines. We're a little desperate, especially for antibiotics, and we're asking everyone to check around to see what they might have. Anything will help.

I looked over at Edmond who was listening in a way that other people listen when they can't quite hear, and I knew he was trying to hear something that wasn't being said. But Osbert said Fine, we'll have a look upstairs and Edmond got up with the rest of them to rifle through drawers to see what they could find in the way of prescriptions so I guess whatever he heard was OK.

This leaves me and Dr Jameson all alone and while he's looking me up and down I'm reminiscing about what a nice time I've had here in England completely free of doctors and what a crying shame it's come to an end so soon, and after a little silence he says, How long has this been going on? And I know he's not talking about the war and I hope he's not talking about Edmond and me, so I say What? like I don't have a clue what he's talking about.

But instead of starting up a big lecture and calling me Young Lady and all the usual crap he just looks at me in a sad sort of way with his tired eyes and says very softly Aren't there enough troubles in the world without this too?

And for once I don't know what to say.

Eventually Edmond and Isaac and Osbert and Piper come back with a whole bunch of half-empty boxes because Aunt Penn isn't much for throwing things away and the doctor looks at them and smiles his tired smile and says Thanks, and then he looks at us all standing there waiting for him to go and pauses for a minute and finally he says Is there anything you need that you don't have?

And we all know what he's talking about and I want to shout NO we especially DO NOT REQUIRE ANY GOVERNMENT-SURPLUS PARENTS THANK

YOU VERY MUCH but I don't say anything and neither does anyone else so he sighs his tired sigh and goes.

Thirteen

Something in the air shifted after the visit from the doctor.

Not exactly because of anything you could put your finger on but if I had to guess I'd say that the magic we were trusting to keep us safe from the outside world suddenly seemed too fragile to protect us forever.

Everyone was quieter than usual that night. Piper and I wedged ourselves into one of the big chairs and were reading *Flashman* together and it was late but still light enough outside to read with the help of a candle or two, and all the windows and doors were open to let the warm air in along with the smell of honeysuckle, and the dogs were dozing near us and Piper suddenly stopped reading and looked at me in her solemn way and said Are you in love with Edmond?

And I thought for a minute about the best way to answer and then I just said Yes.

She stared at me with the Family Stare, the one that normal people don't ever do because it might be considered impolite to crash around in another person's innermost thoughts without their permission, and then she said Well I'm glad you love him because I do too.

My eyes filled with tears then, I couldn't help it. I put my arms around her and we just sat like that with my tears running down into her hair and the night coming down darker and darker and the soft feel of it all around us.

She asked if she could sleep in my bed that night and I said yes and we went upstairs and lay close together in the narrow bed and I wondered if maybe she missed her mother, and then around halfway through the night Edmond came in saying he was lonely and he lay down too only facing in the other direction since it was the only way he could fit, and then around sunrise Isaac wandered in too wondering where everyone had gone and when he saw us he just smiled a little and went down to the kitchen and brought up the big brown teapot and some mugs on a tray and we all piled together on the bed on top of each other like puppies and drank our tea while the sun streamed in thick and yellow through the window.

And it was Edmond, with his oddball sense of what hasn't happened yet, who knew we had to mark that day out as special and he said It's going to be hot, let's go down to the river for a swim.

So we collected our towels and blankets and Piper

packed some food in a basket and we put on shoes and changed out of the shorts and T-shirts we'd been living in every day for weeks and into nice clean ones, and Isaac called the dogs and Piper got Ding from the barn, and then with a feeling of getting a day off from school which may have been totally weird but was how we felt, we set off.

If you climbed up the footpath and walked and walked, up past the lambing barn, along the edges of about six more fields eventually, after an hour, with the little Ding Ding Ding of the bell around Ding's neck for company, you came to a river. Edmond said it wasn't as good for fishing as the part we drove to that first day but was better for swimming because it was deeper. And it ran along the edge of the most beautiful meadow you've ever seen, so full of poppies and butter-cups and daisies and wild roses and hundreds of other flowers I didn't recognize that if you squinted at it from low down it looked like a blizzard of colour.

Next to the river was an ancient apple tree just starting to lose its blossom and Piper and I laid out blankets half under it and half in the sun and then we sat down in the shade to try to cool off while the boys threw off their clothes and leaped shouting into the freezing water and then tried to splash us and called us to Come In Or Else! and finally we got tired of them teasing so we just thought Why not? and Piper took off all her clothes and I took my jeans off and we tiptoed in holding hands, screaming a little and jumping up and down because it was so cold.

Like everyone always says, It's beautiful once you're in.

The feeling of the cold water and the hot sun and having the river just flow over your skin like a dolphin wasn't something I had enough words to describe but was the kind of feeling you never forget.

I got cold quicker than any of the others, who were having races and sitting on rocks by the edge like turtles to soak up the sun before jumping in again, so I got out and flopped down on a blanket in the warm sun and waited patiently while the heat stopped the shivering in my skin and gradually warmed my blood all the way through and then I just closed my eyes and watched the blossom petals fall and listened to the heavy low buzz of fat pollen-drunk bees and tried to imagine melting into the earth so I could spend eternity under this tree.

Then Edmond and Piper came out of the water, Edmond put his jeans on and they both took turns making cold handprints on my stomach which I pretended not to notice, while Osbert and Isaac floated around in the river with the dogs, Isaac humming a melody and Osbert humming the harmony not quite in tune and it was nice for a while to have Osbert be part of our gang instead of the one who always had more important things to do.

Edmond lay down a few inches away from me on the

blanket and lit a cigarette and closed his eyes and after a minute or two I could feel the heat from his body flowing into mine, and when Piper came over with both hands full of petals and threw them up in the air so they drifted down over us both, Edmond laughed and asked What was that for? And Piper smiled her solemn smile and said For Love.

Eventually everyone came out of the water and for hours and hours and hours we lay under the tree and talked and read and occasionally someone got up to throw a stick for the dogs and Piper played with Ding and made tiny woven wreaths of poppies and daisies to decorate his baby horns and Isaac whistled back and forth to a robin and Edmond just lay there smoking and telling me he loved me without saying anything out loud and if there ever was a more perfect day in the history of time it isn't one I've heard about.

The sun waited to go down longer than usual that day so we kept putting off the moment we had to leave and the boys and dogs swam in the river again and eventually we all headed back practically in the dark, dog-tired and too happy to talk much.

I guess there was a war going on somewhere in the world that night but it wasn't one that could touch us.

Fourteen

A few days later we had another visitor only this time
he wore a British army uniform and brought a lackey
with him to take notes and check things off on a list.
He didn't seem particularly interested in us living
without adults, though I noticed him giving Edmond's
burning cigarette a look and I thought Boy oh boy if
you're going to spend any time nosing around here
you'd better be a little more particular about what
shocks you and what doesn't, and then Edmond gave
me a look like Watch What You Say only it should be
Watch What You Think when he's around.

The guy poked around and asked a lot of questions
like how many rooms we had and did the roof leak and
how many outbuildings were there and who if anyone
had been here to see us and I noticed Edmond answered
the question of the outbuildings without mentioning
the lambing barn. Then Mr Regular Army and his
Man Friday tramped off to look at the lay of the land
and came back a while later and said It will be perfect

and boy did I ever NOT like the sound of that.

It turned out that we were being Sequestered which had to be explained to me since I'm not exactly in the habit of having people take over a perfectly private house to send the inhabitants off to live god knows where for The Duration, and all I could think was this would not happen in America but of course for all I knew the Green Beret was already holed up in Bloomingdales.

Osbert was so anxious to look helpful he was practically standing to attention but for once I felt sorry for him because it seemed pretty obvious that we were all going to have to do what they said no matter what, and maybe Osbert was only hoping that somehow he could protect us all by being Respectful. I stuck with what I was good at, i.e. Blank bordering on Sullen and when I looked over at Edmond he had the saddest expression on his face but when he saw I was looking he smiled.

Osbert was the only one with the courage to say what we were all thinking, which was What about us? And the army guy looked up in an absent kind of way that told us everything we needed to know about how concerned they were for our happiness and we kind of drifted off together like a huddled mass yearning to breathe free, no one wanting to lose track of any of the others.

Of course at this point it hadn't occurred to me that

we might be separated, but do you know anyone, even in the middle of a war, who's going to take on a group of five kids especially ones like us who don't exactly remind you of *Little Women* even on our best day?

The army guy went away and said he'd be back tomorrow and afterwards we all stood there shell-shocked if you'll excuse the expression and silent, just in case anything we said out loud turned out to be true.

I started out in bed with Piper that night and as I lay awake with my arms around her waiting for her to fall asleep I wondered if Dr Jameson had anything to do with this, after all it seemed pretty coincidental to have two visitors in less than a week when no one had noticed us for ages. After an hour or so when I was sure Piper was calm and safe I slipped off to be with Edmond and we said even less than usual only climbed inside each other for comfort and oblivion and fell asleep that way wrapped in black sheep blankets and together dreamed a single dream that there was no one left in the world but us.

Fifteen

Every war has turning points, and every person too.

First Osbert went off in the truck with the army guy and came back all beaming with a job, so I guess all those hours learning Morse code and playing spies turned out not to be in vain. I would have been happy for him if it wasn't so obvious that the rest of us had been simultaneously demoted to Expendable Civilian Status and thus were a whole lot less interesting to him. I think he did feel responsible for us in his fashion, but we were way down his list of Things To Worry About what with having the responsibility for saving the world on his shoulders.

By noon the house was starting to fill up with army types and at first we were outraged to see them putting all their stuff into OUR rooms and setting up radio equipment in the barn and moving the animals out without even asking and then we decided the better part of valour was discretion and if we made ourselves scarce they might not get the feeling that we were the sort of kids who needed to be Taken Care Of elsewhere.

We even went so far as to offer them lunch which I'm sure is what the collaborators in France did to the Nazis to keep them happy and I felt pretty much like a pathetic grovelling turncoat even though we were supposedly on the same side. But they said No thank you we've brought Our Mess with us and I wondered why anyone would think it was a good idea to call food Mess. Piper said their food was better than ours, which hardly surprised me given that we'd reached the limit of the number of edible meals you can make with rice and they were eating chicken and dumplings.

So there were Piper and Isaac and Edmond and me Making Ourselves Scarce and just considering whether we should move up to the lambing barn and make ourselves even scarcer when Osbert came out looking guilty and told Piper and me to pack a bag with our things because we were going to be rehoused and I just looked at him and shouted there is NO WAY I'm going to be sent off to some REFUGEE HOME in the BACK OF BEYOND especially BY YOU and Osbert looked pretty miserable and stared at the ground and said Orders Are Orders and I thought It's lucky they didn't tell him to shoot us.

Piper looked from me to her brother like a rat in a trap and then Edmond put his hand on my arm just when I was thinking that maybe if I slugged Osbert it would help him understand I was serious and very very softly Edmond said Don't worry and I said I AM NOT WORRIED because THERE IS NO WAY I AM GOING. And looking at all those miserable faces I wondered whether this was a cultural thing or what, that no one in this country says You've got to be fucking kidding when told to vacate their home and abandon their newly discovered loved ones by a bunch of jumped-up reject army guys playing war games for a lark.

Osbert slid off like a sorry snake and I figured that was the end of it until about five minutes later when some guy who said he was Left Tennant something or other came out and was Awfully Apologetic in an awfully unapologetic way and the gist of it was we were out of here whether we liked it or not. He made it extremely clear that the army was not in any mood to hang around watching some Female American National have a tantrum at this Vital Juncture in History so I took Piper and we went upstairs and packed all the stuff we could think of for a week including some books in case we got stuck with a bunch of local hillbillies, and all I could do was stare at Edmond and Isaac and even Osbert and try to keep from crying and then Edmond kissed me and said Take Jet in a way that no one else except maybe Isaac could hear and I said back I'll find you and he nodded as if to say Likewise.

Our chauffeur wasn't exactly thrilled at me dragging

a dog along but I wasn't budging on this question and he rolled his eyes and said Get In, and then with almost everyone I had left in the world standing nearby looking sad and young and helpless, we were off.

Given how things turned out you might wonder why we didn't make more of a scene about staying together but at the time we figured we could survive a week or two apart.

That's how totally in the dark we were about our situation.

Anyway, we bundled into this open van and as we started off I thought about Ding but I didn't say anything in case Piper got more worried than she looked right now and I did a kind of mental bucking-up because I was Piper's guardian now and I thought I'd better act like it and make it clear to her that she was safe with me no matter what. And the thought made me fierce and strong like a mother wildebeest and all of a sudden I knew where people got the strength to pick up cars with babies lying under them which I always thought was made up.

I took her by the hand and smiled the bravest smile I ever smiled and it was real, even though it might not have been one hundred per cent sane, and it worked a little because she smiled back at me and hugged Jet and started to sing her angel song quietly under her breath.

We drove and drove and I tried to look at the road

signs and follow where we were going but it was pretty confusing and the best I could do was notice the names of villages we went through and hope somehow I would remember.

I started making up a mnemonic the way I used to do in school but it was hard to keep it straight since I had to keep adding words on as we went along, and whoever named these places wasn't doing it with any particular pattern in mind.

We went through Upper Ellaston and Deddon and Wincaster and New Northfield, and Broom Hill and Norton Walton and then I gave up trying to remember and just noticed each one and hoped if I needed them to come back into my head someday they would.

I felt a little pissed off at all those spy shows where the guy gets blindfolded and thrown on to the floor of the back seat and finds his way home by the noise of a chicken here and two bumps in the road there and a dog barking in the key of D which I can tell you now from experience is a load of crap, well who'd have guessed it.

Some of the things that made the biggest impression were the things that were almost normal but not quite.

Like the fact that no one seemed to be outside even though it was a beautiful sunny day, and there were no kids in the playgrounds or riding their bikes along the streets or anything. Also there were no other cars driving and lots abandoned by the side of the road where they'd run out of gas, which took me a while to figure out like What's Wrong With This Picture.

Other things I recognized from our village, like most of the shops either had broken windows or were all boarded up and lots of houses had boarded-up windows too, presumably for when the marauding hordes swept through the Back Of Beyond and wanted to rape all the housewives and pillage their dining-room sets.

And then sometimes there were tanks. Mostly just sitting by the side of the road with someone's head and arms sticking out the top, smoking, and holding on to a gun. In some villages there were lots of them and then for a while you'd see none at all.

About every two or three miles we passed through checkpoints where our driver had to stop and show papers to a bunch of guys with machine guns who didn't speak fabulous English and I thought Oh My God, so there is an enemy after all. They all seemed bored rather than scary and Our Army Guy was very polite to Their Army Guy and I thought it's just as well I don't waste a lot of my spare time trying to figure out this war stuff because if you ask me they're not in the Spirit Of The Thing at all.

We drove for nearly an hour along tiny winding country roads and though judging distances isn't exactly my forte unless we're talking Manhattan city blocks, I figured we'd gone about fifteen or twenty miles by the time we got where we were going, what with speed divided by time equalling four birds in a tree singing 'Melancholy Baby'.

The place we arrived at was a little better than my worst fears which is the sort of thing you have to be thankful for under these conditions and after piling out of the van we were introduced to Mrs McEvoy who lived with her army husband in a newish brick house just outside a village called Reston Bridge and first impressions, while not always right, suggested she wasn't the type to carve us into tiny pieces and feed us to her dogs when the going got tough. But I've been wrong before.

Speaking of dogs you could tell she hadn't quite reckoned on us showing up with one of our own but she took it pretty well considering Jet marched straight over to her pretty little blonde cocker spaniel and started to hump it on the spot.

There was also a four-year-old boy named Albert who they called Alby, and from the room she put us in it was obvious there was an older boy some-where but not here since we were getting his room. We unpacked our stuff and Mrs McEvoy came up and said we should call her Jane and her husband was On Duty and they'd heard about Our Plight and thought it was a Sin to let a Perfectly Good Room Go To Waste when there were Poor Children like us without anyone to take care of us and I had to squint and think of Piper to keep my fake smile from turning into something more like Jason in *Friday the 13th*.

But when I opened my eyes and looked at her again I saw that under all the cheery stuff she looked desperately sad and her face was kind of blotchy like she'd done a lot of crying lately and I thought well, everyone in this weirdo war has a story and hers is probably as bad as any and maybe a whole lot worse.

The sympathy angle got a little strained when she went on about how adorable Piper was and how much she always loved to hear an American accent but after a while I got used to her and thought at least she was trying to be nice which even I had to admit is something.

After having a cup of tea we asked if she'd mind if we just went up to our room and read a book for a while because of being tired from the trip not to mention the war, and off we went to our twin beds under pictures of racing cars and about twenty half-naked posters of some teeny-bop star with cellulite and I thought This room's seen a fair amount of action *à la* Lyle Hershberg and his pet Smurf.

Piper asked if this was where we were going to have to live now and I said I guessed it was for the time being but that once we were settled we'd come up with a plan for getting back together with Edmond and Isaac and she looked more cheerful at that thought and you could tell she was making an effort to make me feel OK about our situation and she said Isn't this a funny place you've ended up in Cousin Daisy, and I said You mean here in Reston Bridge and she said No here in England with me.

And then I looked so far into her eyes that I could practically see out the back of her head so don't ever say I'm not related by blood to the whole telepathic gang of them and I said PIPER: I would have to be buried alive in a ditch and stamped on by elephants before I would ever think that being anywhere with you wasn't a good thing SO THERE.

Then Jane McEvoy called up that there was some food ready and we found ourselves tramping down the stairs like somebody else's well-behaved children and Piper and I just looked at each other and burst out laughing because we'd got so used to being in a world without any sign of adults.

Secretly I was wondering whether these people were going to take care of us or whether we were still all on our own, only now in a slightly different form.

Sixteen

When Major McEvoy came home later that night I accosted him the second he stepped through the door, demanding that he say whether Edmond and Isaac had been moved somewhere else and if so where.

At first he just looked stunned like maybe he'd forgotten he had a fifteen-year-old daughter and then he smiled a little and said I don't think we've been properly introduced, I'm Laurence McEvoy and I thought OK, I can play the Let's Be All Polite Game too and I said very sweetly like the well-brought-up girl I am And I'M DAISY and I WANT TO KNOW WHERE MY COUSINS ARE.

He smiled a little and looked at me in a searching kind of way for a minute, maybe trying to figure out whether I was planning to overthrow the English government with the information I wheedled out of him, and then, I guess remembering that I was just a kid all on my lonesome caught up in the war and we were more or less on the same side, he relaxed a little and he said They've been moved too, to a farm just outside of Kingly which is a Fair Distance East of Here and I'm sure you'll see them again All In Good Time.

I was kind of taken aback by his willingness to breach the Name, Rank and Serial Number stuff and tell me where they were and after that I didn't know what to say except possibly How about showing me exactly where on a map and leaving me the car keys in case we decide to go see them in the dead of night and never come back.

I don't get nearly enough credit in life for the things I manage not to say.

Of course in order to survive, Piper and I needed to have a plan, and I was the one who was going to have to make it because Piper's job was to be a Mystical Creature and mine was to get things done here on earth which was just how the cards were dealt and there was no point thinking of it any other way.

Our major plan, which we didn't even have to discuss, was to get back together with Edmond and Isaac and Osbert by hook or by crook. So far, I was pretty hazy on the details.

I did, however, manage to find a Road Map of the British Isles hanging around the house and look up Kingly and Reston Bridge and what I discovered was that good old Major Laurence McEvoy had told me the truth and Kingly was pretty much straight east of us and not that far from Aunt Penn's sequestered house, though a little further away from Reston Bridge than was totally convenient given the current difficulty in securing a taxi.

The extremely good news was that our very own swimming and fishing river near the house was a branch of the same one that the bridge in Reston Bridge went over and I figured navigation-wise that was a big plus.

It's probably best to say up front that maps are not what I'm good at. So I did what every other sensible New Yorker has been doing for years in the Public Library, I tore the page out and hid it in my underwear. And from then on I always kept it with me Just In Case.

We went to bed early that night and pretty much every other night because without electricity and with even candles getting pretty scarce, there wasn't much point in sitting around in the dark. I didn't much like being in this boy's room with the stupid bimbos on the wall and I know Piper wasn't wild about it or being away from her brothers either.

Before she fell asleep she said Daisy . . .

And I said Yes Piper?

And she said, I always wanted a sister and if I had one I would want her to be like you.

She paused.

Though I always thought she would be called Amy.

I laughed a little then and said It's all right with me, you can call me Amy if you want Piper, but she looked a little hurt and I stopped joking around and said, I practically am your sister now Piper, and that seemed to satisfy her on the subject and she didn't say anything more about it.

I didn't tell her that I had never wanted a sister, in actual fact had spent most of my recent life desperately NOT wanting a sister, but that was only because of the circumstances in which I was likely to get one and besides I never imagined how much I could love someone like Piper though having said that there probably isn't another person anything like Piper this side of Kingdom Come.

She asked me what was going to happen to us and I told her I didn't really know but that nothing could hurt us when we were together. I asked her Do you know what Invincible means? And she nodded because she's read more books in nine years than most people read in a lifetime and I said Well as long as we're together that's what we are.

Then she said in a croaky voice Mum must be so worried about us, and there was something in the silence that followed that sounded so desolate that I went and sat beside her on the bed and stroked her hair over and over and tried not to think about Aunt Penn's whereabouts or whether she was dead or alive. But you had to admit Piper had a point because if I were their mother, war or no war, I'd be half dead with worry by now not having any idea how all my children were doing or even if they were still alive.

Eventually Piper got quiet and I figured she was asleep so I went back into my own bed and started thinking my own thoughts for a while.

Now that I was away from Edmond I could think more or less In Private about all the changes that were jamming themselves into my life and one of the thoughts I had was how you could love someone more than yourself and any worry about getting stuck in the middle of a war and ending up dead was transferred on to worrying about keeping them alive.

This was all confused by the fact that I loved Piper in a protective kind of way and Edmond in a slightly different way, to put it mildly, and given that I had about as much experience with sex and boyfriends as I did with brothers and sisters, it was pretty strange to find myself suddenly overwhelmed with attention from the world's biggest warehouse of magical misfits.

And just to complicate matters perfectly, I was starting to feel responsible for their safety and happiness and got panicked at the idea of them being captured or corrupted by the outside world. Now this was a definite shift from where we'd started which was all about them bringing me cups of tea and holding my hand and exactly when the shift occurred I couldn't tell you.

My head was kind of spinning from trying to clear this up and I wished there was someone I could have asked about it all since I'd never read about any similar kind of situation in all the magazines Leah and I used to buy which I guess either makes me or everyone else on the planet some kind of a freak.

But for once my fate was crystal clear and wedded to Edmond and Piper's and even Isaac and Osbert's so that was that, and I just had to get on with whatever it required of me.

This made me not quite as desperate as I had been and if I lay very still I could hear Edmond thinking about me wherever he was and I thought about him back and then the bond between us was complete.

I guess the difference between Gin and me is that when Gin got shut in the barn she thought Edmond didn't love her any more but because I could feel Edmond out there somewhere always loving me I didn't have to howl all night. Thinking of Edmond like that made the single bed suddenly seem too big so I crept in with Piper who didn't even stir she was so used to it by now and I could hear Jet breathing quietly under the bed.

And so with everything I had left within arm's reach, I was ready to fall asleep too.

Seventeen

Piper and I lived with the McEvoys like people living someone else's life.

Because we were part of an army family we got a much clearer idea of what was happening in England, though a fair amount of it we could have done without knowing due to its not-entirely-cheerful nature.

We spent a couple of days gathering information from Jane McEvoy who liked to talk and was pretty lonely especially since her son was away at school in the north and hadn't been heard of since the first bombs went off and she was desperately worried that something bad had happened to him which seemed fairly likely to me.

I went down to get some water late at night and heard her in the kitchen with Major Mac and he was saying he was certain the boy was safe and We'll all be together again just as soon as this bloody mess is sorted. He sounded amazingly calm and reassuring but I could hear an occasional hoarse gasping kind of cry like an animal choking to death in a noose and when I looked through the door I could see Mrs M. shaking all over and him with his arms around her looking exhausted and patting her over and over saying Now now Love, and I decided to live without a glass of water that night.

The next day her eyes were red but otherwise she seemed OK, and to make conversation she started telling us how proud she was of her husband and that one of Major McEvoy's big jobs was organizing a field hospital for local people because all the real hospitals had been taken over to fix up people who'd been bombed, poisoned or gassed in London. They got shipped out here when the city hospitals ran out of room.

She said that since most of the people out in the country were only dying of appendicitis, childbirth and ordinary Pre-Existent Conditions the field hospital was supposed to take care of them while the more Colourful Cases of War Injury got hospitals with proper walls and beds.

At the beginning, she said, I went to the hospital every day. I read to the patients and played with those poor injured children and tried to make myself useful. But now they'll only let Military Personnel inside due to the security risk. She looked kind of outraged at this and said As if I'm some kind of danger to those people! and Piper and I exchanged a quick glance and we were both thinking the same thing namely, Only if being unhinged is contagious.

Later Major M. told us you'd be amazed at the number of things that can go wrong for civilians in a war. For instance, he said, let's say a kid gets appendicitis or breaks his leg, there was no telephone to tell someone that the bone was sticking out of his thigh, no petrol to drive a car to the field hospital, if you happened to know where it was in the first place, and a big shortage of antibiotics if you did manage to get the kid to a surgeon somehow and wanted to make sure he or she didn't die of infection a week or so later.

He also told us about people with cancer who needed expensive drugs and a pregnant woman he knew with rhesus negative blood whose baby would probably die pretty much no matter what, and old people, some of whom would die sooner or later of strokes and heart attacks or lack of drugs, and some who already had.

Another time Major McEvoy started telling us about the farm problems in the area that he was trying to control and they mostly involved cows who couldn't be milked by electric milking machines once the emergency generators stopped working and had to be milked by hand or they could get mastitis and die. Now there's a side effect of war I bet you never considered.

Once you start thinking about all that stuff that wasn't working it's kind of hard to know where it all ends. Like the incubators for baby chicks not to mention baby humans and electric fences and hospital monitors and those things you use to shock people back to life when their hearts stop and computer systems and trains and airplanes. Even the gas supplies for heat and cooking are regulated by electricity, said Major McEvoy, and how do you think you pump water out of a well?

I felt a science report coming on titled *Electricity, Our Helpful Friend.*

Then there was the problem of burying all the cows and baby chicks and people who died and apparently there were lots of dead things and they were well on their way to becoming a big stinking rotten health problem, but that might have been too much information for me just then, and I thought I wasn't going to eat another hamburger or chicken leg again in a hurry.

The Good Major was also trying to distribute things like milk and eggs and other farm food so all the occupied people wouldn't die of starvation and one or two other tiny details like that so you could say he had his hands full and then some.

I guess by a combination of politeness and osmosis I learned more about farming in the few weeks we lived with the McEvoys than I was ever likely to find out in a lifetime on the tenth floor of an Eighty-sixth Street apartment building where the closest you ever got to Agricultural Produce was a corned beef sandwich from Zabar's with a half-sour pickle which I knew perfectly well used to be a cucumber but how it got to be a Pickle On A Plate was anyone's guess.

Anyway, all this stuff was happening under the rules of The Occupation which never struck me as being entirely clear but as far as I could tell meant you could go ahead and do whatever you liked as long as no one told you not to. I didn't really understand The Occupation because it didn't seem like the kind of war we all knew and loved from your average made-for-TV miniseries.

When I heard how it happened I was pretty impressed by the cleverness of the guys who planned it, who as far as I understood basically waited for most of the British Army to be lured into crises on the other side of the world and then waltzed in and cut off all the transport and communications and stuff so basic- ally they were DEFENDING Britain against its own returning armed forces rather than attacking it.

Major McEvoy said Think about it as a Hostage Situation with Sixty Million Hostages so I did.

I've probably missed some important parts of the explanation but that seemed to be the gist of it and whenever anyone went into more detail I found my brain wandering to things like I wonder if he dyes his hair and Whatever possessed them to choose that colour wallpaper?

There were obviously a few military types still left in England, mostly part of the Territorial Army, which sounds pretty impressive until you realize they're a bunch of moonlighting guys who spend a few weekends a year doing basic training and wishing they were one of the Dirty Dozen. Major McEvoy said it was more or less a Known Fact that the whole situation was temporary and by the time the British Forces could get organized again it would all be over and the Occupiers would be History i.e. dead, but I guess the invaders were trying to Make A Point and had never really expected it to turn out happily ever after for them.

What impressed me was how simple it seemed to be to throw a whole country into chaos by dumping a bunch of poison into some of the water supplies and making sure no one could get electricity or phone connections and setting off a few big bombs here and there in tunnels and government buildings and airports.

We also found out that The Enemy was one reason there was no gas for anyone, since Major McEvoy told Piper and me that Petrol was one of the first things they took over when all the trouble started. The other reason was that you needed Guess What to pump it out of the ground and into the tank of your car.

Eleven letters, starts with E.

I guess it shows the importance of having your own army, even a small leftover piece of an army, because although the Bad Guys snatched up everything they could get their hands on, at least the Good Guys seemed genuinely dedicated to distributing what was left around the place so as few people as possible died from neglect or outright stupidity.

All in all I felt a little guilty about the fact that while us kids had been living the Life of Riley, a whole bunch of other people had been scurrying around like lunatics trying to keep the Social Fabric from Unravelling and my personal belief was there were too many problems to think about and not enough people to sort them out.

In other words, they were desperately short of people to Get Things Done and that gave us a chance to GET OUT and eventually get back to where we belonged. This was obviously our goal, but in the meantime we figured that actually doing something might stop us dying of boredom, which I was starting to realize was a major killer in a modern war.

So for all our making fun of Osbert and his passion to join the War Effort, I could see now that this was our ticket to getting back home.

Or at least that was the plan.

Eighteen

During all this time I was in touch with Edmond. Strange as it sounds, he visited me, not exactly like God visiting Moses or angels telling Mary she's knocked up with the Christ Child, but come to think of it not completely unlike that either.

I had to be in a certain state of mind – quiet, distracted, sometimes half asleep – and then I might feel a kind of aura, a lightening of the space behind my eyes and I'd know he was there. I could smell his smell of tobacco and earth and something radiant and spicy like amber; could feel the smooth glide of his skin, though I never exactly saw him. Once he had a cough, and his breathing sounded slow and heavy. Another time on a cold night when he kissed me I could feel his body shivering against mine. Sometimes I could just feel his eyes on me, holding me with his quizzical wise-dog gaze, and I would push off with one foot and try to coast for hours on that feeling.

Once, in a trance that wasn't quite a dream, an image

appeared in my head and I knew it was the place he and Isaac were living, and I could see the people living with them, and how they passed the time. Another time I heard the frail scratching cry of a newborn baby and Edmond seemed tired and cheerless and disappeared before I could find out what had happened.

Whether I could feel his presence or not, I talked to him constantly, telling him about Piper and Jet and the McEvoys and our life the way it was now, and then in the middle of some rambling monologue I might get the feeling that he was there listening, as if I'd conjured him from thin air, pulled him out of a hat by the ears like a magician's rabbit. I was happiest when he just came and lay down next to me, and I could almost feel the weight of his body against mine. His presence silenced, if only for a few seconds, the crackling anxiety that made my blood grate against my bones and for a little while I'd feel melted and soft.

Don't get me wrong, I'm not about to write a scientific paper about this. I believe in the spirit world about as not-at-all as the next person. I'm just saying what happened.

In retrospect I have to think it was the kind of connection that makes people decide to phone each other at the same instant after fifty years of not talking. You hear about siblings adopted at birth into families thousands of miles apart who both name their first child Vera, dogs that begin to howl the instant their owner is killed in a war, people who dream plane crashes. It's the sort of communication there's no particular reason to believe in under ordinary circumstances and I'm generally not big on ghosts. Ouija boards and black cats are way down the list of neuroses I suffer from.

So you'll understand why I didn't make a big song and dance about my meetings with Edmond. I wasn't even sure I wanted to talk about it with Piper.

I was trying to revamp my reputation. This time around I thought I'd be the sane one.

Nineteen

Before we started angling to get into the wide world again the first question I wanted answered was this whole smallpox epidemic thing.

Major McEvoy looked kind of uncomfortable when I asked him and said It was Not A Likely Danger to the Population At Large at the Present Time, and when I put on my best Shocked Face he said Now Daisy, how would Things Be if there was nothing to stop people wandering around Spreading Rumours and Getting Hysterical and trying to organize raids on The Enemy and that sort of thing, hmmm?

And then he gave me his Name Rank And Serial Number look and changed the subject.

Not being entirely witless I got the picture that if we were going to die it wasn't going to be from smallpox.

What was interesting about this little insight was that I could see the army had a point, but it still seemed like a sneaky trick to perpetrate on all those simple country folk.

With that worry done and dusted I started trying to figure out a way for Piper and me not to spend the rest of our lives rotting in Reston Bridge when we could be out in the world possibly running into some of our long-lost relatives.

So after a few days sitting around twiddling our thumbs and going pretty much stark raving stir-crazy trying to have a sensible conversation while Alby whacked us on the head with a plastic sword every six seconds, we asked Major McEvoy to find us something to do because we were Hard Workers and wanted to Help People which was not a total lie except the people we wanted to help were us. He looked kind of pensive for a minute and said he would think about it and get back to us.

You can imagine that the good Major had a fair bit of thinking to do given that even in the best possible light we were still a fairly useless pair, but then I remembered JET, and that was a STROKE OF GENIUS because a well-trained sheepdog and someone who knew how to get him to do things were just about priceless at the moment what with most of the local farmers dependent on herding their animals with big off-road bikes and there no longer being any fuel.

Piper knew dog-training from Isaac and the two of them were the world's foremost natural Animal Whisperers and could make dogs and goats and sheep, and probably bugs too, do pretty much whatever they asked just by looking at them in a certain way and whistling a little low whistle which for Isaac especially was extremely useful, given the limits of his conversational aptitude.

Major McEvoy kind of perked up at this brainstorm and asked for a sheepdog demonstration. So with a couple of whistles Piper sent Jet out into the garden and what do you know he was off like a shot, crouching down low when he got to Alby and then very gently without being obvious moving him little by little towards us until poor old Alby was standing right in front of his dad looking confused and wondering why every time he turned around to run back out to play Jet was blocking his path.

Piper gave him a pat and looked as smug as she was ever likely to look and I thought YES we are on our way, now if only I can figure out some possible use for me before they stick me in some out-box marked Cannon Fodder.

But it turned out that Major McEvoy was pretty nice after all and also he probably knew that walking off with someone else's pretty nine-year-old girl even in the middle of a war wasn't totally kosher and so he asked me to come along too and I gave Piper a mental thumbs-up sign and she smiled.

It turned out that our place wasn't the only one that had been sequestered and Major M. started taking us every morning to Meadow Brook Farm which was the largest dairy farm for fifty miles in any direction and should have been renamed Fort Knox since the Meadows and the Brooks were teeming with soldiers all trying to take the place of machines.

The problem was, the cows had to go out every day to graze because there wasn't enough hay to feed them and they had to be brought in to be milked twice a day which sounds simple enough until you think about three hundred cows all coming and going, and a lot of army guys milling around the farm like bulls in china shops.

Jet was a miracle to watch in action and he had most of the remains of the occupied British Army in love with him after the first day and Piper was right behind him in their affections. She could get him to separate out ten cows and bring them in to be milked by the army guys and in the meantime have the next ten ready while he took the first ten back.

All the big hunky army types couldn't get over sweet serious little Piper whistling her magic whistle and this black-and-white blur of a dog running exactly where she told him to and she must have reminded every single one of them of their little sister back home or the one they wished they had back home or possibly just the Virgin Mary. Whenever they weren't doing something else they kind of lurked around with moony expressions watching Piper and Jet in action and you could tell most of them felt happy just being near her and that old Family Magic.

Piper acted like she didn't even notice all the attention but I could tell she liked the way everyone asked her serious questions about Jet and treated her as something special. In the average morning at least three or four big guys would hang around for ages and finally get up the courage to say He reminds me exactly of my dog Dipper back home, or How does he know which whistle means what?

But I got the feeling that what they all wanted to say was just You have the most beautiful eyes I've ever seen in my life.

I guess this was fairly obvious, given that she had the same effect on most people, but with all those quirky brothers getting in the way she probably didn't get as much chance to be noticed as you might expect.

The fly in the ointment was that there was too much work for Jet and not enough for me. Having Gin around to help Jet would have solved the first problem and been an all-around godsend but that still left the second. I spent some of my endless hours of leisure learning to shoot a gun, which I thought might come in handy someday, if not in the war then back on the streets of New York. It was a lot harder than it looked but after a while I got pretty good, thanks to all the expert marksmen hanging around disguised as milkmaids.

I tried raising the subject with Major McEvoy of getting Gin drafted into our section of the British Army and you could tell for a minute he forgot that he was supposed to keep us out of trouble and away from thoughts of Regrouping because he just looked sort of absentminded and said No, it wouldn't be possible to get Gin right now because of the Situation On The Roads and also she's probably as useful to Gateshead Farm as Jet is to us.

Thank god I have years of Emergency Deadpan Practice because you wouldn't have guessed that Gateshead Farm meant anything more to me than Porridge Oats but like any good undercover agent I now had two names to put together to make an address and Major McEvoy thought we were still talking about dogs.

I didn't tell Piper just yet because I was hoping for divine intervention about how we were going to get to Gateshead Farm, near Kingly, East of Here, and when.

Back to the dogs. In the end they compromised and managed to find a silly Border collie named Ben, who wasn't much more than a teenage puppy, to work alongside the Master only it didn't work out as well as you might have hoped since he wasn't the brainiest dog on earth and besides was afraid of cows.

It got so that Jet knew his job so well that either one of the army guys or I could take over some of the time while Piper tried to train some sense into dim Ben, practising over and over again until he was just this side of useless. He still ran away bleating if any of the cows took it into their heads to look at him sideways, but most of the time they couldn't be bothered and he managed to muddle through.

Sometimes I caught Jet giving him a look that was totally unimpressed and I could almost see Jet thinking Excuse me, but who invited this blockhead to the party?

And sometimes I wondered if he might be thinking the same thing about me.

Twenty

Now you might have gleaned from some of the hints dropped so far that food was not my best subject. So it was kind of ironic that the part of the army I got enlisted into was the one trying to provide it for everyone.

There was the whole milk operation, starring Piper and Jet The Wonder Dog, and the part that came after milking was complicated by having to heat and sterilize the milk since there were no fridges to keep it cold and that turned out to be so hard that eventually they gave up and just served it the old-fashioned way straight from the cow. Everyone worried about un-contaminated containers but the best solution turned out to be making people Bring A Bottle, then at least the army knew the milk was OK when it left them and if it poisoned anyone later it wasn't their fault.

There were a couple of local guys who knew all about butchering so they were the lucky ones who got to kill and divvy up the cows which was a lot bloodier than you might want to find yourself thinking about on a dark and stormy night. They were popular though, and suddenly had whole bunches of friends they'd never noticed before, queuing around the block clutching barbecue tongs.

Chickens were having their necks wrung all over the place especially if they didn't keep churning out eggs, and it was pretty surprising to me how many of the older folks seemed to be right at home strangling a chicken. Piper said it was because of the Last War and rationing and everyone keeping chickens and I was pleased to hear that some of the skills I was picking up would stand me in good stead in Later Life, assuming I had one.

And finally, anyone who was healthy enough and willing enough to pick crops was hauled in to help and that was where I came in.

My first job was picking Early Apples, which was somewhat more useful than hanging around on the outskirts of the Piper Appreciation Society. I got a lot of doubtful looks at first about whether I was strong enough to work so hard but these days determination was nine tenths of the law and also as time went on there were a lot more thin people around and I didn't stand out so much.

I worked with eight other army people including three soldiers and their wives and two other civilians. We started early in the morning and worked until it started to get dark and after only a few hours we drifted into cliques like we were all back in school.

My partner was a local woman called Elena who was from Liverpool originally so I didn't understand most of what she said for the first few days and vice versa. Eventually we started chatting about this and that and soon the stories started coming out and I heard all about how she and her husband Daniel met and what were their favourite movies and how often they had sex and though she was a lot older than me and we barely spoke the same language she turned out to be the kind of person you could talk to about pretty much anything without worrying that she'd report you to the Pope.

She wanted to know all about my American and English families even though she'd never met any of them except Piper, and how I'd ended up picking apples in the middle of a foreign country not to mention the middle of a foreign war. Sometimes I thought I might implode if I didn't talk to another human being about the events of my new life, especially the parts someone my age wouldn't be allowed to see in the movies. But every time I was just on the verge of pouring it all out to Elena I changed my mind at the last minute just in case.

Luckily it seemed riveting enough to her that I was American and had been sent over by my Evil Step-mother which got her all clucking and tutting and all I had to do was look kind of tragic and say nothing at all for a few minutes and suddenly I had a new best friend enlisting the whole bunch of apple-pickers into hating Davina on faith, which cheered me up for ages.

When we started work they gave us big boxes to pack the fruit in and the basic trick was not to throw the apples in or they would bruise and rot and ruin the rest of them in the box which suddenly made sense of the One Bad Apple expression my teachers trotted out all the time, or Two if you counted Leah.

We had baskets, and ladders you had to move whenever you ran out of apples close enough to reach, and when the baskets were either full or unbearably heavy you passed them down to one of the others and they unpacked the fruit carefully and passed back empty baskets. It didn't seem to matter whether I was picking or packing because both jobs were equally tiring, and the first few days I had to lie on the ground for twenty minutes at a time to keep from passing out from exhaustion and the pain in my arms. Elena was nice about it and just kept working around me.

It was such hard work that at first I thought I wouldn't be able to stand it, what with every muscle in my body aching and me hardly able to climb into the truck or get out of bed the next day. But I did it because pushing myself further and further past what was possible made me feel calm, which is hard to explain but something I was good at.

One of the guys who worked with us was a few years older than me and I didn't like him much but unfortunately the feeling wasn't mutual. He was called Joe and he started hanging around trying to get my attention by telling stupid jokes while we worked and asking totally duh questions like What's it like being a Yank? Elena felt sorry for Joe due to him not being the sharpest knife on the rack, especially when it came to picking up rejection vibes, but it was easier to feel sorry for him if you weren't being eyed-up like prey.

Maybe he's lonely, she said, and I just looked at her wondering if she expected me to open a Home For The Socially Challenged or what. Then she started giggling and I had the feeling we were thinking the same thing, namely, some people are lonely for all the right reasons.

After that we both pretty much ignored him.

Most of the workers except Piper, Jet, a few others and me lived at Meadow Brook so we were picked up every morning at seven and taken home at seven every evening and every night we fell asleep in the truck and just about managed to wake up for some food and climb into bed and that was our day.

It took a lot of getting used to but after the first week we compared muscles and I told Piper all about Elena and it almost made up for the fact that when we had a day off neither of us got out of bed at all. Even Jet didn't seem interested in moving out from under the bed except when we called him for food.

The plums turned ripe at about the same time as the apples and sometimes we moved from one to the other just to vary the routine but it was easier to strip a tree of apples because they were less fiddly and you didn't have to move the ladder so often and when the plums fell off the trees they rotted and attracted thousands of wasps so Elena and I stuck with apples when we could.

Elena was what you might call a Big Girl and you could tell she wanted to ask me about being so thin but being English she would rather have sawed her own legs off at the knees. I caught her looking pretty puzzled a few times when she saw me nibbling at bits of lunch when everyone else was wolfing down anything in sight and I could tell, war or no war, she was thinking If Only I Had Her Self-Control.

I found out she'd been trying to have a baby for seven years and was smack in the middle of some special last-ditch treatment when the war broke out and she couldn't get any more treatment now and was forty-three and didn't know when she'd ever get another chance.

I told her she should borrow Alby for a few days if she wanted to appreciate how great it was to be childless but when I looked at her she was just managing to smile and her eyes were kind of bleak and I wished I hadn't said anything at all.

After about ten days of picking some of us moved over to broad beans and that was worse because you were always bent over with a whole new set of aching muscles but at least the beans tasted nice when you got them home and cooked them. It was getting to a point where there wasn't much around that tasted of anything you'd want to eat and even I had to say I could do with a nice piece of toast which made Elena laugh.

One night we were driving home through the usual checkpoints and Piper and I were asleep and Joe, who sometimes came with us to stay with his parents in the village, suddenly took it into his head to stand up and get show-offy, and I guess thinking war was some kind of open discussion forum where everyone was really interested in your opinion, started shouting a whole bunch of obscenities at one of the checkpoint guards and when Major McEvoy told him to sit down in a really icy army tone of voice he ignored him and kept shouting stuff about Johnny Foreigner being an Effing Bastard and worse.

And then in an almost lazy kind of way the checkpoint guy who'd been looking at him raised his gun and pulled the trigger and there was a loud crack and part of Joe's face exploded and there was blood everywhere and he fell over out of the truck into the road.

Piper watched the whole thing without moving a muscle but the shock of it made me retch and I had to turn away over the side of the truck. Someone else was screaming and when I turned back the whole world seemed to have slowed down and grown quiet and from inside the silence I watched the guard go right back to chatting with his friend and saw Major McEvoy's head roll back for a moment and his eyes close and a look of despair crumple up his face and in that split second I wondered whether he was really that attached to the kid and then it was with horror that I looked down and saw that Joe was still alive, gurgling and trying to move the arm that wasn't caught under his body and when I looked back at Major M. I realized he was doing what he felt was his duty as a member of the armed forces defending a British national and still in slow motion he was climbing out of the truck and his plan must have been to get Joe on his feet somehow and then to safety when I heard about a hundred shots from a machine gun and the momentum of the blasts hurled Major M. backwards across the road away from Joe with blood welling up in holes all over him and this time you could see Joe's condition was a hundred per cent dead with brains splattered everywhere and our driver didn't wait around to see what might happen next but just stepped on the gas and as we drove away I thought I felt tears on my face but when I put my hand up to wipe them it turned out to be blood and nobody made a single sound but just sat there shell-shocked and all I could think about was poor Major M. lying there in the dust though I guess he was much too dead to notice.

There never were seven more silent human beings in the back of a truck, we were too stunned even to cry or speak. When we reached Reston Bridge our driver, who

I knew was a close friend of the Major's, got out of the truck and stood there for a minute trying to get up the courage to go inside and tell Mrs M. what happened, but first he turned to us and said in a voice that sounded broken and full of rage, In case anyone needed reminding This Is A War.

And the way he said those words made me feel like I was falling.

Twenty-one

We had plenty of opportunity to notice that poor old Jane McEvoy seemed to have lost a good number of her marbles already over the past few weeks and it was obvious that this was going to be the last straw by a pretty substantial margin.

Piper and I tried to occupy Alby while she crashed around the house wailing with grief and army wives kept arriving to console her like such a thing was possible and Alby, who didn't get at all that his father was dead, kept playing his favourite game which consisted of Bashing Things and then Bashing More Things and then Bashing Anything That Was Left. After about six hours of Bashing he ran out of Things and started to grab on to his mother and howl which just made everything worse.

Major McEvoy's friend and driver Corporal Francis, who everyone called Frankie, went with a couple of other guys to try to retrieve the bodies but they couldn't get near the checkpoint due to warning shots being fired at anyone who approached. When he came to stay at the house that night I tried to talk to him about getting Mrs M. some sedatives but I never saw a person look tireder or more dispirited than him and I got the feeling he was already doing so much more than his best on so many fronts that digging up a prescription for Valium would be his last straw, and anyway he was the one who could've used a few hundred milligrams.

Piper and I scraped together something like an omelette with a few eggs and some of Alby's milk and we cooked some beans from the farm and cut up some plums and we gave most of it to Frankie who didn't eat much and Alby who did, and then we put Alby to bed and went to bed ourselves right afterwards leaving Frankie with Mrs McEvoy and two of the army wives crying in the kitchen which by this time was almost totally dark.

That night was bad and Piper kept jerking awake wide-eyed and shaking and saying she kept seeing the face of the boy who got shot and then she started to sob and say she wanted her mother and I'd just get her calmed down and asleep and it would start all over again. When I thought about Joe I felt fairly bad that he got his head blown off but mostly furious that because of him being such a fool Major Mac had to die.

When I finally got to sleep I found Edmond and told him everything that happened, and he stayed with me for hours and whether I was dreaming or just borderline schizophrenic I didn't know and didn't care either.

At around six a.m. when everyone was still sleeping four soldiers came bursting into the house looking for Frankie and said we had to leave immediately, that a vigilante group had started up and they went in the night to ambush the checkpoint soldiers and now The Enemy was going house to house and killing anyone they didn't like the look of.

All hell broke loose.

Mrs M. stayed frozen in one position like she didn't understand English or even how to walk any more but everyone else was shouting and running. I tried to talk her into getting Alby, but she didn't even look at me and then Frankie took over and told me to get dressed and I grabbed some clothes and two warm blankets and told Piper to take one of Major M.'s sweaters and save a place for me in the truck and then I stuffed a few useful things inside the blankets including a jar of olives from the pantry and a jar of strawberry jam which was just about all that was left in there and as I was looking around for anything else that might come in handy I saw a silver compass on a little plinth with Major McEvoy's name on it and an inscription, and feeling like a grave robber I smashed it on the floor to pull it loose and the compass came off and I stuck it in my pocket along with the little knife I had from fruit-picking.

I assumed Jet would just follow us into the truck, but when it came time to leave there was no sign of him, maybe because of all the noise. Piper looked stricken and whistled and called with her voice getting higher and more hysterical and much as everyone wanted to see a little girl reunited with her dog there was no way they were going to risk everyone's lives waiting for it to happen so I pulled her in beside me and we drove off without him.

Piper didn't even cry, but just sat there looking completely blank which was worse.

We all sat dazed and speechless in the truck, Alby quiet for once and Mrs M. still frozen, and we drove south according to my compass and only stopped once to pick up some of the army guys I recognized from Meadow Brook and who could just cram into the back with us.

Other people tried to flag us down as we drove along, the sound of a truck these days was enough to get people running out of their houses to see what was going on, and some of them tried to get us to stop by standing in the middle of the road or jumping on to the side of the van but Frankie just said in a low voice to keep our heads down and he kept driving and didn't even slow down.

Piper and I were hanging on to each other feeling stupefied with fear and loss and Mrs McEvoy was holding on to Alby like a drowning person and Alby just sat there thrilled that he was going in a car and could see all the trees rushing past him and as the tears streamed down Mrs McEvoy's face faster and faster I thought Her husband's dead and maybe her older son too and now she has to leave her house and all she's got left is one drooling kid without any idea what's going on and she didn't even think to bring him some milk.

We drove for ages until we got to a big barn with lots of army trucks parked around it and everyone got out and Frankie said We'll stay here for a while and we went inside and it was a huge hay barn filled with guns and sleeping bags and all the signs that the army was using it as a barracks and Piper and I found a corner of the loft that didn't have anyone else's stuff in it and put our things down and then sat down and waited to see what would happen.

Alby was having a fine old time running around looking at everything and the only thing we could do that was useful was to try to keep him away from the guns that were just lying around. I wasn't about to have him blow himself to smithereens on account of it would clearly be the end for his poor old deranged mom.

As the day went on the army guys kept coming and going and they all seemed to have some sort of plan like ants in an anthill going about their business in a nice orderly fashion until a foot comes along and stamps on the whole structure.

Piper and I slept a little and we found some

magazines hanging around and borrowed whichever ones didn't feature extremely obscene pictures of naked women, which were few and far between. And eventually Piper said in an apologetic way that she was a little bit hungry and she went off to see what she could find and came back with half a loaf of bread which was about as easy to get hold of these days as a piece of the True Cross and she also had some cheesy stuff they called curd and it tasted pretty good.

Early in the evening the soldiers started coming back from patrolling The Locality in groups of three or four and some of them came over and told us what it was like out there which as far as we could tell wasn't very nice what with all those laid-back enemy troops suddenly getting aggressive and diving into action which generally seemed to involve killing people like us whenever possible.

I obviously didn't think this was a good thing, but it did coincide a whole lot more closely with my understanding of what a war was supposed to be.

Anyway, lots of them talked to us or recognized Piper from the farm and nobody said Where's Jet? or What happened to Major Mac? because we were all catching on to the fact that some questions were better not asked.

Piper and I were thinking more or less the same thing, namely, first we were five plus Jet, Gin and Ding and then we were three with Jet and now we were just two.

If you haven't been in a war and are wondering how long it takes to get used to losing everything you think you need or love, I can tell you the answer is no time at all.

Twenty-two

It was strange sleeping in the barn with all those soldiers and it felt a lot less safe than you might have thought, given how many guns were around. It probably had something to do with realizing that the Bad Guys might want to find out where all the Good Guys were sleeping and then ambush them. But there wasn't a whole lot we could do about it.

Piper and I had a little corner with a kind of overhang that made us feel protected and we put down the two blankets and rolled up some clothes for a pillow and as a last thought I went to see if Mrs McEvoy and Alby were OK and warm enough and yes, they were warm enough, but not OK. I sat and tried to talk to Mrs M. for a while but it didn't do much good because she seemed to have lost track of everything in the world and whatever words I could think of to say just came out sounding stupid.

I couldn't stay with her too long in case her

desperation rubbed off so I made an awkward excuse and climbed back up into the loft.

Piper and I huddled together under the blankets and it was noisy and busy all around us as the soldiers made some food and cleaned up all their weapons and yelled jokes at each other across the barn most of which you couldn't repeat, and finally they turned down the hurricane lamps and in shifts they slept too, with a watch that changed every few hours. It wasn't the best night's sleep I've ever had but we were getting used to strange circumstances and it wasn't the worst either.

One of the army guys called Baz, who we knew from milking, came over to us in the morning with some oatmeal and milk and cups of tea and we were so grateful and he was so in love with Piper that he sat and stayed with us while we ate and told us As Much As He Knew.

He said that the murders of Major Mac and Joe had sparked off a nasty battle in that area and it was exactly what everyone had been trying to avoid. The Enemy apparently wasn't any more anxious than we were to start fighting and shooting, and they had proved it by letting our army get on with whatever they had to do for the better part of three months.

But no one was happy now, and there were a lot of stupid brave Country Folk armed with duck-hunting rifles taking potshots at tanks and most of the time getting slaughtered for their trouble.

Baz was smart and trying to be funny to cheer us up and said we shouldn't worry and found some trashy paperbacks for us to read while we were hanging around all day. He said he'd come see us that night after he got back from patrol.

When he did come back Piper was off helping the cook and I took the chance to tell him about my plan to get back together with Piper's family though I swore him to secrecy, and he looked pretty worried at the thought of us setting out alone but didn't actually say the words Don't Be Crazy which was moderately encouraging.

I asked if he thought it was possible Isaac and Edmond and Osbert were all still living together and he shrugged and said Anything's possible, but there's a lot of trouble about. He looked at me for a minute like he was trying to size up what I was likely to do and finally said No place is really safe. You're better and worse off here with us . . .

He stopped for a second but then pretended he'd just been distracted by a noise and started talking again.

. . . but if you did set off alone and kept off the roads and away from obvious danger you might be OK. The trick is to avoid contact with anyone you can't positively identify because everyone's tired and up against the clock and most of The Enemy know they're never going home again and don't have a heck of a lot to live for.

He stopped again.

This time it was because he saw Piper coming back from the cooking area with some soup and she smiled her beautiful smile when she saw Baz and folded herself down into the straw, leaning up against him like a cat to eat her supper.

One thing you sure couldn't miss was how many strange alliances were forged in a war. You could see Baz was as happy as he'd ever been in his life just sitting next to Piper, war or no war, and not in a creepy way either. You could just tell that after months around nothing but big smelly burping farting men, the presence of Piper with her big eyes and pure soul made him feel like all he wanted was a chance to die to protect her. I didn't seem to have that effect on anyone but it would have been a waste for both of us to be saints.

That night Baz moved his sleeping bag from across the loft where he'd been all along and laid it across our corner. Hours after I fell asleep, I woke up to see him half-sitting, awake and watchful. And the way he occasionally looked over to make sure we were safe reminded me exactly of Jet.

Twenty-three

For almost a week we stayed like that, bunked up with various members of the Territorial Army. Piper seemed to go inside herself more than usual but for me it was just one more chapter of my increasingly surreal Normal Life and I had a calm feeling most of the time, like nothing could happen any more that would surprise me.

Except for Mrs McEvoy we were the only females in the barn with over a hundred men and they acted like we were the Queen and Princess of Sheba, bringing us food and coming over to talk and play cards and generally treating us like prize mascots or holy relics when in fact we were two grubby kids surrounded by soldiers in a dusty place without windows waiting for the war to catch up with us.

Most of the soldiers were so much more normal and friendly than you ever would have expected back in the olden days before everyone in your entire circle of friends and acquaintances had something to do with the army. I guess they were just regular people who probably never expected to get drafted when they signed up as part-timers. Most of the time you got the feeling they were lonely and fed up and wanted to go back home to their other lives as much as we did.

Since there wasn't much to talk about except the war, I kept asking them all questions about camping and surviving in the wild and finding food and all those kinds of things and I doubt they gave a whole lot of thought as to why I was so curious about survival skills since most of them loved to talk about the subject at length anyway.

Piper and I weren't encouraged to go outside much so we read a little and helped in the mess and slept. It wasn't so different from being back at the McEvoys' except there were lots more people to talk to, and with all that time on my hands I couldn't help wondering why life in a windowless barn thousands of miles from America surrounded by soldiers felt more real than most of the real life I'd ever lived.

We got used to sleeping with Baz guarding us, and being brought food, and having shy twenty-year-olds sidle up to us and start up awkward conversations just for something to do. Even the noises of all those men around us, not all of which were exactly suitable for polite company, got to be reassuring in a certain way.

Baz seemed to get a special status from being Piper's minder and after that first day the two of them fell into a kind of brother and sister thing that I'm sure came from the fact that almost every relationship in Piper's life up till now had been with all those brothers. Baz was more normal than any of the ones she had at home, but he had something of that watchful stillness I associated with her gang. Birds of a feather find each other, I guess.

Well obviously all this Girl Scout Happy Families stuff wasn't going to last forever.

At about four in the morning a few nights later we woke up to the noise of a lot of scuffling and shouting and Baz saying Get all your stuff together and Stay Here and then him disappearing into the chaos and us not being able to see anything much because there were no lights but then there was gunfire and then he was back and leading us out through the stable door back where the latrines were and he took our stuff and told us to follow him and we ran and ran until I thought my sides were going to rip open from the pain and I kept tripping because there was no moon and it was blacker than black and finally we got to an open space and we just stood there panting and Baz said Look you can see the sky getting a little lighter over there, that's east, just keep walking in that direction and use your compass to find NNE, not NE, he said, Or you'll overshoot.

I was glad to know this fact because being from New York City where everyone's born knowing uptown is north but not a whole lot else, I didn't know anything about NNE versus NE and was glad someone had let us in on that secret.

By now Piper realized Baz was leaving us and was starting to cry and he picked her up in his arms like she weighed nothing more than a handful of hay and just held her as tight as he could and finally he kissed her cheek and said Daisy will take care of you and he winked at me behind her back like we were in cahoots which I guess we were.

Then he gave her one last squeeze and shoved a heavy package into my hands and before I had a chance to see what it was he was running back in the direction we came.

Come on Piper, I said, let's keep going while it's still darkish and we can find someplace to hide and then we'll rest when it gets light.

And as we walked along and the noises of guns got to sound like little pops I told her about knowing where Isaac and Edmond were staying and having a map and talking to Baz about my plan and pumping every soldier in the barn for clues on how to survive in the wild. Piper seemed pretty substantially cheered up by all this surprising information and I said Once the sun starts to come up we'll look for a place To Bivouac and we both burst out laughing at my use of technical Boy Scout terminology and I said Honestly! That's what it's called.

Now here's a good time to explain that footpaths are

god's gift to people trying to travel long distances without using roads. I guess in America we'd have to crash a path through the woods but here it was all nice and civilized and half the time they were even marked with little arrows leading to gates to climb over and even when we left the farm and moved into much more open ground without fences you could still see indications of paths.

We felt like we were about a thousand miles from any other human being and even though it had been a cold night, by about eight thirty a.m. when I thought it was time to find someplace to hide we'd been walking for hours and the sun was up and we were starting to feel warmed through.

The path we followed was fenced in on one side by stone walls covered in blackberries and other thorny bushes and there were smallish trees just beyond and though most of the undergrowth wasn't higher than a few feet, it got pretty dense pretty quickly which kept us from straying.

We were completely clueless about how safe we'd be walking around out here. One of the soldiers I'd talked to said there were hundreds of people heading into the countryside away from the action in order to try to disappear and wait out the trouble which suggested it would be like walking around in a shopping mall. On the other hand I got the feeling that there were more than enough footpaths in England to go around

and the average refugee wouldn't be interested in social-
izing. The soldier's theory was that most of the people
we were likely to meet would be English people but
he also said That doesn't mean they won't shoot you
on sight.

I couldn't really believe that a whole bunch of enemy
soldiers were going to spend their spare time crashing
around in the undergrowth looking for stray people to
shoot but it still seemed like a good idea to keep a low
profile for as long as possible or at least while you were
pretty sure the world had lost its mind.

As the sun got hotter we decided to stop and rest
and we found a nice dry piece of ground about fifty feet
off the path that was pretty much out of sight if you
were sitting or lying down which is what we felt like
doing anyway.

The package that Baz gave me started out heavy and
was getting heavier by the minute and I was glad to put
it down and figure out how to untie the covering and
find out whether it was worth lugging around. Inside
were all the things we probably should have thought
of taking along with us and hadn't, like a plastic bottle
full of water and some flat bread and a pretty big piece
of hard cheese, some salami, matches, a big folded-up
lightweight plastic sheet, a nylon rope, a little metal
bowl. And a gun. I wrapped the matches and the gun
back up in the bag for emergencies and added the
rest of the food and other things to our blankets and

supplies, namely the olives and strawberry jam, which was about the extent of it. To cheer us up on our first day on the road I made jam sandwiches for breakfast and they tasted hopeful.

We drank some of the water and with the sun getting hot we lay down in the grass for a rest and if we hadn't been on the run going god knows where we would have been pretty happy. After sleeping for a while, we collected blackberries and ate them and then because it was so incredibly silent all around us except for the birds and bugs we decided to set off again in the light of day because although it's a great theory to travel by night, it's a lot easier said than done if you have no idea where you're going and there's no moon. Trying to follow the path and watch the compass all at the same time was proving difficult enough in broad daylight since the path headed slightly south-east and we wanted to go NNE but I figured we'd just have to try to swing up to the north when we got a chance.

One thing there was no shortage of was blackberries, and for lack of anything else we ate handfuls of them, which made your stomach feel pretty bad but they tasted good so we didn't care.

We walked for four or five hours and as the sun got lower we started looking for a place to spend the night and once we thought we saw a house but it was almost burned to the ground with only one wall standing so we gave it a wide berth. The temperature dropped fairly quickly now that it was September and although it wasn't exactly cold, we weren't exactly SAS troops either and I didn't think we should be stuck out without shelter so we stopped while there was still a little light and managed to tie the rope from a tree to a stick we jammed as deep as possible into the ground like a peg, and hung the plastic over it and weighed the edges down with stones. It collapsed about a hundred and fifty times before we managed to get it strong enough to hold when we crawled in with our blankets, and it was uncomfortable, but we were used to lying on the ground and also pretty exhausted and managed to go to sleep.

It rained a little during the night but we stayed mostly dry and some of the rain ran down into a curled-up corner of our tent, and we slurped it straight out of the plastic in the morning to save the water in the bottle and because we were so thirsty. We'd both been bitten by something or other in the night and it didn't improve my mood to have a face covered in itching welts and wild hair and no toothbrush and also to feel so grubby from not having a bath in ages. I was glad I was too thin to get my period because that would have pushed me over the edge.

We packed up all our stuff and this time I made it into two bundles. I carried the big one and Piper took the small one and with the bundles slung crossways on our backs it wasn't as bad as you might think and anyway we weren't exactly pressed for time.

We walked and walked and walked and the path swung up to head more north than south which was a big relief, and when it started to rain again we stopped to rest and tried to get all our stuff and us under the plastic sheet and collect a little rainwater in the bowl at the same time.

Piper and I had been together for so long now that we barely talked any more than we had to. We were tired and hungry and lost and our feet hurt and there didn't seem a whole lot to say and I was very glad she wasn't the type of kid to ask stuff like Are we there yet? because There Yet wasn't a notion I felt up to addressing at the moment.

So we rested. Then we walked some more. Past another burned house. Past a child's shoe abandoned on the path. We kept walking. Then we rested. And walked. We didn't see anybody but there were signs they'd been there. Discarded clothing. Paper. A dead cat. We ate some of the food and drank some of the water and only occasionally wondered what the hell we thought we were going to find at the end of the road.

We could have kept going for another hour or two but around mid-afternoon we saw something that looked like a falling-down hut and it was a little way off the path and hadn't been burned so we climbed over the wall and crashed our way through the tangled thorns and grass until we got to it and it was big enough to lie down in and fairly dry inside though it smelled like rotten wood. We felt as relieved as if we'd suddenly come across a five-star hotel and before the rain started up again we collected armfuls of long grass to make a nest that was nearly soft enough to rest on comfortably and then I opened up our two back-packs and laid the blankets out and it was amazingly cozy and actually pretty civilized if you didn't count the spiders.

Piper was out picking flowers to put in our new home like we were going to stay there for years and suddenly she shouted Daisy! and my heart stopped and I shot over to where her voice was coming from and she said Look! And when I looked I didn't see anything but a shrubby tree and papery acorns underneath it and she said Hazelnuts!

It was lucky Piper was my faithful companion just then because I wouldn't have recognized a hazelnut if it tapped me on the shoulder and asked me how to get to Carnegie Hall but we collected a shirtful of them and then smashed them open on a rock and ate as many as we could without throwing up and I found myself wondering why hazelnuts weren't everyone's idea of five-star cuisine.

When we'd eaten about a thousand of them we collected as many more as we could and cracked them open and put them in with the rest of our provisions and had a few olives and some bread and then blackberries for dessert.

Then with nothing else to do except notice how hungry and thirsty we were and how much our blisters hurt we went to sleep and only woke up when the world started crashing with thunder that sounded about six inches above our heads but amazingly our little hut turned out to be watertight enough so that if you stayed away from the left side and stuffed the plastic in a certain way through a hole in the roof you didn't get soaked and could go back to sleep. Also the rain seemed to discourage the bugs which was an unexpected plus.

In the middle of the rainstorm I remembered our bowl and reached out to get it, filtered off the stuff that was swimming on the top and drank the water down. Then I put it out again and in only about ten minutes it was full and I woke Piper and told her to drink it while we had it. After four bowlfuls of water each we both felt a lot better except for stomach cramps I guess from the cold water or maybe the nuts and I filled the water bottle and went back to sleep.

When we woke up again it was still raining and there didn't seem any point in moving from our happy home until we had to. It seemed like an incredibly bad idea to get our few clothes and blankets wet given that we didn't have any others.

Piper was looking dreamy and seemed happy enough

lying under the blankets singing to herself and I decided I was desperate to get clean so I used the bowl full of cold water and the rain to try to have some kind of bath which wasn't very effective especially with no soap. Then I came back in and got dressed and huddled up to Piper to get warm again and for a while we played an incredibly convoluted word game called Mental Jotto that involved trying to remember how many letters of all different words were in the word the other person was thinking of and it was exactly complicated enough to pass the time.

She had just guessed Skate which was right and now it was my turn to guess but after a minute or two of trying Bacon, Cable, Deary there was no answer so I said Piper? but she was sound asleep. I lay there for a while listening to Edmond's voice in my head and it was calm and familiar and a little bit wistful and I started to relax and forget about everything but him and that was another day gone.

Twenty-four

Now here's a really amazing fact: my eighth grade math teacher actually turned out to be right about one thing, namely that someday I was going to need to know the answer to the question where X = Piper and Daisy, and Y = four miles an hour, and Z = carrying a twelve pound load, and N = a north-north-easterly direction, and 4D = four days.

So now go figure how much closer to Gateshead Farm did X (Y+Z) + N × 4D make us? It goes without saying I hadn't been paying attention that year.

Our footpath crossed over four single-track paved roads but except for a cow grazing by one of the roads we hadn't seen another creature bigger than a hedgehog. There was the occasional barn and once a row of little houses but they looked deserted and we didn't want to risk finding out for sure.

The path seemed to switch directions constantly but overall we were now headed more or less in the right direction. Though for some reason I kept remembering a show I saw on TV about navigation in whaling ships and how the tiniest error could mean you missed the island you were aiming at by five hundred miles.

At one crossing we could actually see a road sign that said STRUP – 1/4 MILE and EAST STRUP – 1/2 MILE. I was so excited at getting a bearing that my hands were shaking almost too much to open the map, but when I did look more or less where I thought we should be there was no sign of anything like Strup and Piper said There might just be a couple of houses so it's not worth putting it on the map.

For some stupid reason I started to cry then and I felt completely choked with despair and worthlessness and I couldn't believe I was trying to lead Piper miles across England to find something the size of a microbe on a map when in my real life I couldn't even find a clean pair of underwear in a chest of drawers. But unfortunately no one else jumped up and volunteered to take over and the way Piper just stood there holding my hand and waiting for me to stop crying made me buck up and start walking again.

After the hazelnuts we found an apple tree and more blackberries but the chances of coming across a nice steak sandwich seemed remote and our food resources, which had started out running low, were now within a stone's throw of the bottom of the bucket. At least it was raining on and off so we didn't run out of water but it made walking slippery, and wet sneakers rubbing on blisters isn't my favourite feeling so that was about the extent of our good luck.

We stopped for lunch that day around eleven in the morning and couldn't even spread out a blanket to make an event of it due to the ground being wet so we had to perch on rocks, when either of us would have given anything to stretch out someplace warm and dry, and I was unwrapping our last piece of cheese to eat with a few olives and the end of our nuts when Piper said Daisy? And when I looked at her she said What's that noise?

And I listened and listened but didn't hear anything at all. But she had that look on her face that I knew from Isaac and Edmond and I knew she was hearing something and I just hoped to god it wasn't something horrible when her face suddenly burst into a thousand watt smile and she said It's the river! I'm sure it's the river!

And we left all our stuff and ran down the path and sure enough about a hundred yards further down it came to the river and when we looked at the map we were pretty sure it was OUR river and if we could just manage to follow it without getting too waylaid it would take us more or less exactly where we wanted to be.

Then we did a little dance and whooped and laughed and hugged each other and ran back to our supplies and packed them all up again and set off feeling light-footed instead of just light-headed for the first time in days and we walked till sundown and then camped near the river.

It wasn't particularly warm but we got undressed and dipped ourselves in the water to wash anyway and for the first time I noticed how skinny Piper was which once upon a time I would have thought was a good thing and now I thought was just what happens when you're nine years old and don't have enough food to grow properly.

As the freezing water flowed around us we rubbed the dirt off our bodies and without dirt both of us looked white as ghosts with farmer's tans on our face and neck and arms. Against the whiteness you could see every mark standing out in bright red hieroglyphics telling the story of our journey. Both of us had feet covered in raw and half-healed blisters and raised scratches on our arms and legs from being too tired to hold back thorn bushes that got in our way and insect bites we'd scratched till they bled and nettlerash pretty much all over and I had a wide scrape on one knee that was weeping pus and made me limp because it hurt so much to bend it. Aside from that we were both covered in bruises from sleeping on stones and being too exhausted to get up and rearrange things once we were lying down.

We got out of the water shivering like mad but more or less clean and tried not to look at each other because it was too depressing to acknowledge what we looked like and we stood for a little while in the cold evening wind to dry off because it had become kind of a fanatic compulsion to keep our blankets dry.

So much for the healthy country life.

The next day we set off again and the path followed the river and after half a day of walking, the river forked off and checking the map we knew for the first time since leaving Reston Bridge EXACTLY WHERE WE WERE.

And that was the second time I cried and Piper laughed and told me to stop wasting water, but I couldn't because it was for relief and disbelief in equal amounts and although knowing where we were told us fairly clearly that we hadn't made nearly as good progress as I thought we had, at least we were going in the right direction and knew where we had to go next.

The map showed we had twenty miles to go, and once when I went on a Five Boroughs Sponsored March against poverty or something, I walked twenty-two miles in one day and I wasn't eating a lot more that day than this one.

That night I slipped into the place in my head where I could talk to Edmond and for once I had good news.

Twenty-five

Following the river changed our lives instantly for the better. We knew roughly where we were headed and I didn't have to spend hours juggling the compass and the map and living in a panicky limbo wondering if somehow we'd gotten turned around and were heading to Scotland or Spain by mistake.

Also knowing how far we had left to go helped with figuring out how much food we could eat and though we were no better off than before, at least we didn't have to worry about making half a jar of strawberry jam and a couple inches of salami last another month.

Piper kept finding field mushrooms and saying they were perfectly safe to eat and up until now I thought it was a bad idea in case she was wrong and we got poisoned but she seemed so sure and there were so many and I was starting to think if we didn't have something different to eat we might die of despair even before we died of hunger so we decided to cook our first meal of mushrooms and salami and here's how we did it.

First we set up our so-called tent and waited until sundown so no one would see the smoke, then we collected some dried dead weeds and made a pile of them and next to it a pile of twigs and little bits of branches that were completely dead and dry, then we got some stones from the river bank and made a circle and saved a few stones that we could balance our little metal bowl on, then we lit the dry weeds with one of our matches and waited till they caught and then added twigs slowly, and although it took two tries and four matches and the twigs weren't as dry as they should have been, we had a pretty nice fire going after about twenty minutes.

It must be some well-known phenomenon that if you stare into a fire when you're already half out of your mind due to a variety of deprivations you will immediately find yourself hypnotized. It took a supreme effort of will to pull my eyes away from it and if I hadn't done that, Piper and I might still be sitting there today, gazing into the flames and feeling the heat on our faces and hands, triumphant about making something as wild and effective as a fire, even though we did start out with matches which was obviously a lot easier than rubbing sticks together.

I left Piper staring into the flames and cut a smallish piece off our chunk of salami then chopped it up into even tinier pieces and put them in the metal bowl and because the salami had so much fat in it, it started to melt immediately and then I took about six big cut-up mushrooms and a few of the little blue ones Piper said were called blewits and added them slowly to the bowl with the fat and the little pieces of meat.

I made a cover for the bowl out of a piece of bark that started to smoke at the edges and burn, which made it hard to take off so I could stir the mushrooms, and I burned eight out of ten of my fingers getting the bowl off the fire so the mushrooms wouldn't burn and it took almost an hour of doing this but eventually the pieces of mushroom looked small and brown and then we waited for them to cool and you wouldn't believe how something you found in a field could taste so good especially with the little pieces of salami which were salty and a little burned and crunchy.

And as I started to eat the pieces of mushroom I suddenly thought All this time I've been starving, and without noticing I said it out loud, so that Piper said So have I, without even looking up and I thought No you haven't, not in the same way and I hope you never are.

We finished the mushrooms and then washed the bowl in the river and mixed a couple handfuls of black-berries with some strawberry jam for dessert and then washed the bowl again and made hot water over the fire which we sipped and pretended was tea and for an hour or so we felt full of good warm things and happy.

Then we put out the fire and went to bed.

*

About two or three hours after we fell asleep I woke up to find Piper sitting up next to me wide awake with a look of naked terror on her face. I sat up too but couldn't see or hear anything and I just said What? What's happening? but by that time Piper had started yelling and I practically had to smother her to shut her up because I was so scared of someone hearing us.

She was thrashing around like a person having a fit and trying to claw my face with her hands and I thought maybe she was suffering from some form of mushroom poisoning. NO! she screamed and I thought she meant me but her eyes weren't focused outwards at all even though I was trying to put my hand over her mouth and she was shouting STOP STOP!!! and I was concentrating on her so hard that the noise in my head when I finally heard it too took me completely by surprise. It started softly like a throbbing noise far away and for a second I looked around like mad, thinking it must be near us, but all around was quiet and empty except for nature and the night.

Gradually over the throbbing I could make out something like a tape played too fast so the voices were all squeaky and odd like cartoon alien voices and then I started to pick out individual noises and then I could hear people crying and screaming and by then the voices were so loud and so desperate and it was so horrible that I could only hug my head and beg them to STOP STOP STOP.

Piper wasn't screaming any more and just lay curled up on the ground with her eyes squeezed shut and her hands clamped over her ears and she looked so terrified that I forced myself to go over to her and try to help but she kicked and hit me when I came near so I backed off and she just rocked herself back and forth like a crazy orphanage baby trying to comfort itself.

All this time the noises were screaming louder and louder in my head and I had to get away from it but nothing worked and all I could do was make a kind of droning noise in my throat to drown it out and after a while it started to fade and got fainter and fainter and eventually the throbbing noise went too and it was silent all around us again and I threw up.

Piper finally opened her eyes and crouched up on her knees and she looked at me panicky and wild like a cornered animal and said We have to help them!

And I felt angry and said Help who? thinking we're the ones who'll need help if we're going to die in the woods from mushroom poisoning. But Piper didn't answer and just kept saying We have to help them We have to help them, over and over like a desperate tape on a loop.

There was no moon at all that night and no point trying to walk because the darkness was so black we couldn't even see the path and though Piper was frantic to get going, even she realized it was useless until we had some light.

We tried to go back to sleep but it didn't work and so we waited trembling in the cold night air until it started to get light enough to walk and then we walked and walked and didn't stop until nightfall when we collapsed and didn't even have the energy to put up our tent but just put the blankets down on the ground and I kept thinking I could feel bugs crawling on me and stones under my bones and Piper half went to sleep but kept waking up with a jolt and finally just when the sky was starting to get light we both fell asleep, like vampires.

A few hours later we woke up sweaty and anxious and once more walked as fast as we could, given how exhausted and starving we were, in a kind of hollow desperate silence.

Neither of us mentioned the mushroom night again.

It was two days since we'd come to the bend in the river and I figured if we didn't get lost, another day of walking should get us to Kingly.

I tried not to think about what we would find when we got there.

There was no point letting my brain get there first. It might decide to turn back.

Twenty-six

Our footpath finally came to an end on a winding paved road just wide enough for a single car. The road was sunk deep down with high banks on either side and hedges on top of the banks so it was like standing in a ten-foot trench with a low grey lid, which was the sky.

Birds were zooming in and out of the hedges singing and squawking and probably wondering what we were doing here since the wild world had been mostly theirs for months now. Neither of us liked being on a road all exposed so anyone could drive up behind us at any time because there was no place to hide without scrambling up a ten-foot slope. But along with being nervous there was a secret feeling of exhilaration to think we might almost be SOMEWHERE.

From the map it looked like we were less than a mile from Kingly, but unless we found a nice policeman or a friendly milkmaid to give us directions to Gateshead Farm, we didn't have a clue what road it was on or where to find it.

We walked about a quarter of a mile past a handful of empty boarded-up houses, and came to a signpost that pointed towards Kingly and Hopton and Ustlewithe so we just kept walking hoping for the best when what do you know, the next turning had a faded wooden sign on it saying it was called Gateshead Lane and by now Piper and I were almost running. No matter how I tried to calm down I couldn't stop the hope and excitement in my chest making my heart crash against my ribs and Piper seemed unnaturally flushed.

After about half a mile we thought maybe it wasn't the right road after all, but we kept going because there was nothing else to do and finally there was a sign and a gate and a couple of farm machines like threshers marooned in mid-thresh and the nervous excited feeling I had began shifting into something anxious and dark as we walked through the gate because I did not for one second like the atmosphere of the place.

You couldn't really see the farm from the road but we saw a lot of birds flying around to the left so we walked forward carefully and finally came around a bend and saw the main barn and still no signs of life and now all I wanted to do was run away as fast as I could because you didn't need to be a child genius to get the feeling that all those birds were circling around for a reason.

I'd been imagining what we'd do if the farm had been taken over by The Enemy and Isaac and Edmond and everyone were taken prisoner but I had to pretend they were still alive because there's no way any person with an ounce of sanity is going to walk on starvation rations for almost a week believing in the possibility of bad news.

You don't always get a chance to choose the kind of news you get.

Put yourselves in our shoes for a minute, walking into this deserted place on a glowering grey autumn day when it should be filled with animals and people and life but what you find is nothing, no sign of people, just the eeriest lack of noise possible and nothing moving except the big black birds in the air and legions of crows standing absolutely still, watching us.

And then we see the foxes.

My first thought was that they were beautiful, sleek and well-fed and vivid orangey-red with sharp little intelligent faces and it didn't occur to me till second thought to wonder why there were so many of them and why they didn't run away.

Well why would they? It was paradise. Dead things everywhere and when the stink hit you it was like nothing you ever smelled before and when you hear people say something smells like death trust them because that's the only way to describe what it smells like, putrid and rotting and so foul your stomach tries to vault out through your throat and if your brain has any sense it wants to jump out of your skull and run away as fast as possible with or without the rest of you so it doesn't ever have to find out what's making that smell.

Having come this far I didn't know how not to keep going. My legs kept walking forward and when I got a little closer I could see that some of the bodies were human and then a kind of coldness came over me and no matter what I discovered I wasn't going to scream or cry or anything.

I was ice.

The birds were pecking at a dead face in front of me, tugging at the skin and using their beaks to pull jagged purple strips of flesh free from the bone and they flew up into the air for a few seconds when I waved my arm so I could see what was left of it and by that time I knew from the size of the body and the clothes that it couldn't be Edmond and if it couldn't be Edmond it couldn't be Isaac and it wasn't Osbert either.

There were more bodies.

Seventeen in all that I could see, and only one I thought I recognized. I was pretty sure it was Dr Jameson and the shock of seeing someone dead that I knew set off a new attack of panic. My legs started to shake against each other so hard that I had to squat down in the dirt to keep from falling over.

One by one.

One by one I approached the bodies, nice and methodical, saw how dead each one was and sometimes how young, and one by one each turned out not to be the person I most feared it would be.

They were all over the farmyard and all looked like they'd been running away, or crouching down trying to hide, or protect someone else, and when they still had faces you could even see the looks of fear and dread at least in the shape of their mouths because the eyes and lips were the first things to go. I started out trying to scare the foxes away from the bodies and I ran at them crazy with rage but they barely seemed to notice me unless I actually kicked them and then they retreated a few steps still holding on to whatever body part they were biting and looked at me dispassionately and I'm sure they could tell I was afraid.

Altogether I found nine men, three women and five children. One of the children was a girl, younger than Alby, still with her mother's arms around her. The woman looked young, but like all the women was fully dressed in dirty and blood-stained clothes so whatever funny business you expect in a war hadn't happened here other than murder in cold blood.

As for how long ago they died, I couldn't tell. Long ago enough, I guess, for their insides to start rotting and the crows and foxes to call all their friends and family round for a party.

Beyond in the covered paddocks were the animals, mostly cows and half-grown calves, nearly a hundred of them crammed together with no food, mostly dead but a few still standing and some lying down making a harsh moaning kind of noise when they breathed and when I took a few steps closer clouds of birds launched themselves a few feet into the air and then settled right back down again and went back to pecking and fighting over the best parts and now that I was a little closer I could see the rats crawling out from inside the dead animals and foxes tugging at stinking intestines exposed through holes torn in the flesh and a feeling came over me that if I didn't get as far away from there as soon as possible I was going to start screaming and never stop.

I started to run and heard myself panting with panic and I looked around for Piper who was nowhere to be seen and I yelled PIPER PIPER PIPER barely drawing breath or giving her time to answer and there was no sign of her anywhere and the hysteria rose like the sea until I was drowning in it and I ran into the only place left which was the barn and there she was just kneeling there tears streaming silently down her face with her arms around an animal and it wasn't until I heard a faint ding when it moved that I realized who it was only I never would have recognized him because he was covered in shit and as thin as the thinnest thing that could still be alive and I guess he'd been left in there with no food for much too long and his eyes were dull but he recognized Piper and me and dinged his bell and rubbed his baby horns against Piper as best he could given that he was mostly dead.

Ding.

He was too weak to stand up and too sick to care about the water Piper brought him.

So I covered him with a grain sack and shot him in the head.

Then I took Piper back home.

We didn't even bother camping but just walked along the road as fast as we could with the strength we had left, scrambling into the bushes whenever trucks went by and staying there until it was safe.

It was never really safe. There were men with torches and we heard shouting and the trucks were passing pretty often and under different circumstances we might have felt scared.

We made slow progress.

We didn't speak but I held Piper's hand and told her over and over that I loved her through the blood beating in my veins and running down through my hand and into her fingers. Her hand started out limp and cold like a dead thing but I willed it back to life until after hours of walking the fingers started to grip mine, a little at first and then harder, and eventually I knew for sure it was still alive.

At sunset the sky cleared and turned orange and grey and pink and the temperature started to drop but to compensate there was a bright moon so we wrapped ourselves in our blankets and kept walking and following the map and what with all the stopping to hide and occasionally to rest it was nearly morning but still dark when we came through the deserted village, past the pub and the village shop, and started up the familiar long hill to the house. I expected the landscape to be barren and dead but it wasn't. The hedgerows sagged under the weight of life: berries and flowers and birds' nests. The optimism of it should have cheered me up a little but it didn't. It was like seeing a vision of some past life, a life so recent and so distant that I could remember the exhilaration without being able to remember what it felt like.

In my new incarnation, I expected nothing, good or bad.

The house looked deserted, dark and silent, even the honey-coloured stone had the feeling of something abandoned. The old jeep was parked off to the side where we'd left it when the gas gave out. There were no signs of life.

No signs of death either.

I wish I could say my heart soared at the sight of it but it didn't. What heart I had left no longer felt like flesh and blood. Lead, maybe. Or stone.

I told Piper to stay outside and she sank down with her head cradled in her arms while I crept in and looked around but I didn't have the energy or the courage for a room by room search so I went straight to the pantry and in the back of a low cupboard found a can of tomatoes and one of chickpeas and one of soup and a glass jar labelled Chutney that even people practically starving to death in a war wouldn't touch but at least it was food. I smashed a hole in the top of the can of tomatoes and gave it to Piper who sucked out the juice and handed it back to me to finish.

Then as the sun started to come up we made our way slowly, wounded and exhausted, to the lambing barn.

There must have been thousands, hundreds of thousands, millions of places in England that hadn't been touched by the war: the bottoms of lakes, the tops of trees, the far corners of forgotten meadows; little remote corners where no one ever went in peacetime because the place wasn't important enough or on the way to anything else or no one could be bothered to ruin it.

The lambing barn was one of them. Although it was early October there were still enough leaves on the trees to hide it completely from the path, and the blood froze in my veins until we pushed through the overgrown path and saw that it was still there.

It was still there, despite all the death and disease and misery and sadness and loss everywhere else. Inside it looked mercifully untouched. No one had been here since the night a thousand years ago that we all slept together, happy.

The good news was that we'd been too lazy at the time to lug everything back to the house so there were blankets still laid out on the hay, and even a few clothes the boys had left behind – T-shirts and spare jeans and socks, worn back in a universe where you wore things once and then put different things on.

Exhausted as I was, I said to Piper that I had to make sure there was nothing left of the smell of yesterday anywhere on my skin, so in the pale weak sun of early morning I rubbed myself all over with freezing water from the metal trough and put on a pair of Edmond's jeans and a T-shirt and though there was nothing left of the smell of him on them I felt better wearing his clothes. I couldn't face the filthy sweater I'd been wearing every day to keep warm and although the new clothes were a little musty, when I crawled in between the wool blankets and put my head down next to Piper's I felt almost clean and safe and best of all, home.

That night I slept the deep dreamless sleep of the dead.

Twenty-seven

We could have moved back to the big house but we didn't.

Maybe it was too close to the road or maybe we'd turned a little wild and couldn't live in a normal house any more. Whatever it was, we stayed up at the barn doing nothing but sleeping for almost three solid days at first, only getting up to finish off the rest of our provisions and for water and to pee in the bushes.

And then when we'd slept enough but needed a fire and something to eat, I suddenly remembered the basket Isaac brought to the barn that we hid from Piper five months or was it five years ago.

Even at the very worst times it had never occurred to me to pray but I did now.

I prayed that the mice hadn't invaded the feed bin. I prayed that the food hadn't all rotted in the summer heat. I prayed to all the gods I never believed in my whole entire life that there would be enough for Piper and maybe some left over for me.

I guess this means I now have to believe in God.

The cheese was hard and mouldy on the outside but otherwise fine and there was lots of it. The fruit cake stayed perfect in the tin and the apple juice was fizzy but not totally undrinkable and the dried apricots were fine, as was the huge thick slab of chocolate wrapped in brown paper. The only thing I had to throw away was the rotten ham, which smelled enough like the awful smell at the farm to make me start retching again.

Clear October nights were turning into clear October days and though it was cold in the barn, it warmed up outside by mid-morning and Piper said it was because the earth still held the heat from summer. So we laid our old blankets against the south wall of the barn and sat in the warmth of the stone wall like old ladies, drinking fermented apple juice watered down with rainwater to make it last, breaking off small pieces of cheese and fruit cake and trying to eat slowly so we didn't throw up from the shock of real food. It tasted almost too rich to eat and made our stomachs feel dizzy and we just sat there not moving, trying to repair our brains and our bodies with slow swallows of food and water and with peace and idleness and familiar surroundings.

After a few days like this we went to bed deciding that the next morning we would walk back to the house and see what we might find there so I guess that meant we were turning back into something human again.

In the middle of that night I woke up and heard

something rustling down below us in the barn and my first thought was Edmond! and my second was Oh god here we go again and my third thought was that maybe it was a rat and we should check that the food was safe but there was something about the way it sounded that was familiar and as I went to sit up I saw Piper's eyes suddenly wide open and awake and the first smile I'd seen on her face in so long and she whistled in a soft way and The Thing gave a little yip and I almost laughed out loud being the last one to realize it was Jet.

We raced down to him and he was much thinner with a ragged-looking coat but otherwise he seemed fine and happy to see us and he just lay there on his back in the most undignified way, wriggling with pleasure as we rubbed him and hugged him and kissed him and told him how much we'd missed him.

Then I left Piper with him and went over and got a chunk of cheese and one of fruit cake out of the feed bin and fed it to him as slowly as I could though it didn't seem to matter since he wolfed it down without chewing and it was only not knowing how long we were going to be living on this food that stopped me giving him all of it, he seemed so hungry.

We were too excited to sleep and neither of us wanted to let Jet out of our sight so we half carried half dragged him up into the loft which he wasn't exactly wild about but in the end we all three lay down, Jet a little separate from Piper and with Piper's hand around his front paw for security and me with my hand around Piper's front paw also for security and that's how we slept.

The trip down to the house took a lot of strength, physical and mental, and we didn't have much left. Without saying anything I braced myself for the worst and what we found wasn't the worst, but the house was pretty well trashed and it was a little like being kicked again when you're already down.

The lights and telephone were still out. There were no messages, no notes, nothing that told us where to find Edmond and Isaac but on the good side there were also no smashed windows or shit spread around on the walls just for the sake of it. A lot of the furniture had been thrown out in the barn and most of the rest was shoved into the corners of rooms or turned upside down and there were broken dishes everywhere and the ones that weren't broken were caked and filthy and the toilets were overflowing and there was mud and dirt all over the rugs.

The kitchen was the worst and I guess even army guys like to spend lots of time in the kitchen and the big table was covered with heaps of paper. There were maps drawn on the wall and no food except what I'd found in the pantry that first day and when Piper and I went to check the barn next door there was no sign of the chickens or sheep or any other animals, which didn't tell us whether they'd been set loose or taken away or served up to the army for lunch.

In the main bedrooms things were a little better with furniture just pushed to one side and fairly clean. I had to hold my breath before opening the door to my little room but stepping inside I was surrounded by those walls pure white and centuries old and everything pretty much the same as the day I left except the daffodils dead and papery in the bottle. I picked up a blanket from the floor and smoothed it on to the bed and looked out the window at the world outside and remembered arriving in a jeep with Edmond.

I could still hear our voices in the walls.

Before I went out I opened the little chest of drawers to find clean clothes all neatly folded and right then I forgot about everything except wanting to be clean. I guess the only reason our clothes hadn't been touched was that they were too small for anyone to have bothered with.

In the hall I looked in the big mirror which was a mistake because for a minute I didn't recognize the person I saw there, including how thin I looked and how dirty and how matted my hair was and the next thing I did was to check the water in the taps which it turned out didn't work without the pump. Piper helped me lug buckets of water up the stairs from the water butt in the garden and I filled the bath a little way and with a bar of Aunt Penn's soap, a bottle of shampoo and a room full of clean clothes I started to reinvent myself as a person.

If you've ever worn the same clothes day and night for weeks, you'll know how amazing it feels when you make your skin silky and smooth again, and how happy you can be just cutting your fingernails and scrubbing the dirt out of your hands and feet with good soap that smells like roses and then putting on clean clothes and brushing your CLEAN hair and letting it dry all soft and whispery-sounding in the sun.

We filled it again for Piper's turn in the bath and then she made me go up to her bedroom to choose some clothes for her because she didn't want to go herself. I don't know what she was scared of but she was adamant that she wouldn't go, in the way little children are adamant that there might be something hiding in the closet in the dark. I guess she was scared of the ghosts that were creeping all around the house and I couldn't blame her.

I picked out some clothes for her including a clean white shirt, which I knew was completely impractical but the luxury of being clean and impractical was too much to resist. I also packed a bag with sensible things like jeans and sweaters with hoods and underwear, and socks to wear at night on our hands and feet in case of bugs.

When we were both clean and dressed in new clothes and had moved the furniture back where it belonged as best we could in the sitting room we felt pretty cheered up. I think the best feeling was throwing away the filthy sneakers I'd been wearing every day for months now and putting on a pair of loafers from my previous life that felt new and expensive and smelled like leather.

We had to do something about Jet because he kept biting at the burrs stuck in his coat but he was definitely against the idea of a bath and the best we could do was find his dog brush in the mud-room and take it up to the barn and try to clean up the tangled mess of his coat which didn't please him much either. We also took a bag of dry dog food that was still in the pantry because feeding ourselves was enough of a problem without having to figure out how to feed Jet. It was heavy and a pain to carry but neither of us knew whether he could manage for himself catching squirrels and rabbits.

Back up at the barn I carefully stowed our booty: matches, soap, clean clothes, more blankets, dog food, a single candle I found under a chair, and some books. Collecting anything more than that would have required a second trip and when you're tired and underfed, two miles cross-country feels like more than enough.

That evening Piper disappeared while I was still sitting outside in the last warmth of the day and after a while I went to find her and she had gone on her own into a corner of the barn wrapped in a blanket hugging Jet and was crying almost silently, her nose and eyes red and swollen and her mouth open as the tears flowed out of her like a bottomless well.

I didn't have to ask why she was crying. The fact that we were clean and more or less safe just made the absences more glaring and for all my longing after Edmond at least I'd come to terms with losing my mother a long time ago but all Piper had left out of a mother and three brothers was me, a dog and a whole lot of unanswered questions.

I wanted to tell someone that this was it, the end, I couldn't go on any more with my own misery plus Piper's, which was so much worse. I felt full of rage and despair, like Job shaking his fist at God, and all I could do was sit with her and stroke her hair and murmur enough, enough, because that's what we'd both had.

Twenty-eight

We couldn't go on. We went on.

Staying alive was what we did to pass the time.

Ages ago I learned in Social Studies about how the Cavemen and the Bushmen and other Primitive Tribes spent every waking hour searching for food and it was nice to be able to draw a good straight line through history between Hairy Old Neanderthal Man and us. I was thinking of approaching my old school next time I was in New York and telling them to replace the unit on Media Communications with one on How To Survive Half Dead In The Wild Without Much In The Way of Hope.

Luckily there was a fair amount of stuff around to eat just now, it being autumn, the season of Fruitfulness and Thanksgiving, but I won't pretend it was an interesting diet and I could have killed for a grilled cheese and tomato sandwich on rye and a Diet Coke, which come to think of it was pretty radical for me and if only one of my thousand shrinks was here to pat himself on the back and take the credit.

Anyway there were lots of potatoes because in order to get to the barn you had to walk along an entire field planted with potatoes and though the army guys living at our house had obviously noticed this too, there are still only so many potatoes a small platoon of hungry sequesterers can eat in a month especially without any of the essential ingredients for mash, French fries or potato salad. In other words, we still had about nine tenths of a field left to eat.

I spent most mornings digging potatoes and carrying them back to the barn to store in the feed bins while Piper went off searching for natural morsels like watercress and sweet chestnuts and honey. As usual, she cornered the Wood Nymph market while I settled for Old Faithful.

Some days when I couldn't bear to dig up another spud, I went with her, and seeing Piper in full flight you realized that whoever the father of these kids was, he had to be some kind of bona fide pixie. She knew how to follow honeybees back to their hives and then how to get honeycomb out of them by making a torch out of a green branch so it smoked and the bees either flew away or got dopey enough to let her break off a chunk of the comb without stinging her, but to be safe I watched this operation from as far away as possible.

One day she showed me about getting watercress out of a river and explained that you had to get it out of a RUNNING river otherwise it would destroy your liver. What about a meandering river I wondered to myself. This is one of the things I most dislike about nature, namely that the rules are not at all precise. Like when Piper says I'm pretty sure that mushroom isn't poisonous.

Anyway I didn't really know what to do with a big fat sticky dripping honeycomb or a couple fists full of watercress other than sending them to some factory where they'd be wrapped up in styrofoam and plastic, but amazingly they tasted just like honey and watercress without having to do anything at all to them and what with digging up potatoes as well, I was starting to think that except for the deli counters and five or ten thousand other total essentials, supermarkets were pretty much a waste of time.

In the meantime I learned the hard way to store things like honey in a tightly covered container if you didn't want to get every bug on earth flying in for a taste.

Piper could smell wild garlic and onions in a meadow and she came home with armfuls of the stuff, which we shredded up to make potatoes with wild onions and garlic for a change from potatoes without wild onions and garlic. There were days I would happily have traded the entire future of England for a single jar of mayonnaise but unfortunately the opportunity never arose.

We roasted sweet chestnuts in the fire and they were pretty good except incredibly hard to peel and the skins got under your fingernails and hurt for days. I spent practically a whole afternoon collecting chestnuts and when I got back Piper looked at me with as close as she ever got to contempt and said Those are Horse Chestnuts and Inedible.

There were a few rows of sweetcorn in Aunt Penn's vegetable garden, along with whatever cabbages hadn't been eaten by the British army and the slug army, and also a fair number of squashes, some leeks and beans and mint running wild.

I brought a heavy frying pan up from the house and because we had no cooking oil we steamed vegetables in water over the fire. Piper said we should catch a rabbit and kill it for the fat to cook with but when I looked to see if she was out of her mind she got kind of defensive and said That's what the *Boy Scout Handbook* says.

A few days later Piper said we should try a fishing expedition and the thought of it made my heart sink because of our Perfect Day and not wanting ever to go there again and ruin it, but nostalgia wasn't a big part of the decision-making process these days so we got Piper's fishing rod and set off.

It was cloudy and drizzling which Piper said was good for fishing and as usual I watched while she lured food on to the bank, but once she caught anything I had to follow her directions about killing and cleaning it while she turned her head away. I had no complaints about Piper but I could have lived without ripping the guts out of dead trout to save her from doing it. Not to mention whacking them over the head with a club in the first place. I hated doing it but I COULD do it and I guess that was the difference between us.

Later there was poached pink trout that made most of the things you eat in life taste gross by comparison, followed by hazelnuts mashed up with honey and afterwards we had mint tea and it was nice but you couldn't help lying awake at night thinking about toast and butter.

In the days that followed we figured out how to make soup from whatever we could add to a pot and that was much better than just boiling things one by one. Leek and potato was the best and when we ran out of leeks we used wild onions.

We set as much as we could store aside. There were only two feed bins in the barn built to keep out mice and I'd already stacked one with potatoes and the other halfway with nuts and corn and cabbages. What we really needed was a huge Amana Fridge Freezer with ice-maker and root beer dispenser.

One funny thing was that I didn't look much different now from the day I arrived in England but the difference was that now I ate what I could.

Somewhere along the line I'd lost the will not to eat.

Partly I wouldn't be good old Daisy if I didn't get my appetite back just when everyone else in the world was learning how to starve, and partly the idea of wanting to be thin in a world full of people dying from lack of food struck even me as stupid.

Well what do you know?

Every war has its silver lining.

Twenty-nine

I knew Edmond would come back to us if he could.

I tried doing the thing they do with dogs in the movies, saying JET FETCH EDMOND! and pointing in the general direction of the Wide World but he didn't bound off like Lassie following a hot scent, just sat down and stared at me politely for a few seconds and then lost interest when it turned out I wasn't going to clarify my request.

Can't you at least send Jet to look for Gin? I asked Piper in a What Kind of Dog Whisperer Are You tone of voice. But she shook her head and said He'd find her if he knew where to look.

We both looked over at him sitting with his nose slightly raised into the breeze.

See, Piper said, he's keeping tabs on the neighbourhood. All the smells from miles around are filtering past his nose.

I came across Piper deep in conversation with Jet one afternoon and when I asked her what they were talking about she shrugged and said Dog Things. Sometimes the loneliness of being the odd man out in these conversations got to me but most of the time I just ignored it. I like old movies. She talks to dogs.

As the days passed and there was no sign of Edmond or Isaac I had to fight the unbearable fear that always lurked at the back of my mind. It took a long time to admit that I could no longer feel his presence and sometimes I lay awake until dawn listening desperately to the silence and trying to remember his face.

Sometimes I thought I heard Edmond's voice in my head but it always turned out to be my subconscious replaying old tapes out of some perverse kind of nostalgia.

I denied what appeared to be fact.

And yet, I had seen the dead people. I had looked carefully at every hideous, nightmare face just to be sure.

I found myself drawn more and more to the big house just to make sure Edmond wasn't waiting for us there, or had managed to drag himself that far but no further.

I made excuses to Piper about being gone for a few hours, or just told her I'd found something in the vegetable garden that would be ripe any day now like late tomatoes or maybe we needed something like more clean socks. She didn't mind my going alone because she didn't much like going there herself on account of the ghosts and also she probably more or less knew why I was going and was glad to have someone checking on the off chance.

She always took Jet with her for company so I had no early warning system and every time I approached the house I searched for portents, strange cloud patterns, thirteen magpies, frogs the size of antelopes, that sort of thing. Some days I was convinced I could sense something or I experienced an uncanny mystical feeling, but it won't make the six o'clock news if I tell you I was always wrong.

It didn't matter. Each time my heart would race at the smallest suggestion that we had company. Usually it was a moth thudding against a window. Or mice. Or nothing at all.

Once there I tried to put things back where they belonged.

I moved furniture. Swept rugs. Washed plates with cold water and bars of soap. Scrubbed dirt off walls.

Sometimes I just sat in my little room or the room Edmond shared with Isaac, hoping something would happen.

Sometimes I put on his clothes and drifted around the house looking for something but I didn't know what.

I frightened myself. I became the ghost Piper was so scared of.

One day we went down to the house together because Piper wanted a bath. There was no use pretending I had a premonition when Piper was around because if any manifestation was going to make itself manifest, it wasn't going to be to me.

We had to haul buckets in as usual and the bath was cold but at least it took place in a bathtub, and then we sat around for a little while in the garden and swapped books we'd read for unread ones and I guess it was a little like going to a movie in the olden days before the war, something different to do.

For a while there was total peace and quiet, with nothing but the sound of Piper humming quietly and a Chiffchaff chiff-chaffing in the apple tree and me turning the pages of a book.

Then the telephone rang.

It was such an unfamiliar sound we forgot how to react.

For an eternity neither of us moved.

Piper sat terrified. Eyes wide.

But I've never left a ringing phone in my life and I wasn't about to start now.

I brought the receiver up to my ear but said nothing.

Hello? said the voice and for a moment I couldn't place it.

Hello? it said again, and then in a pleading tone:

Whoever you are, please say something.
And then I recognized the voice.
Hello, I said. It's Daisy.

Part Two

One

I ended up in a hospital, where they kept me for months after I arrived back in New York, staring at a wall, stunned silent, frozen rigid with anger and grief. My willingness to eat confused and annoyed the staff, confounding their efforts to understand what I was doing there. For months, an explanation for my presence escaped them completely. But I wasn't about to help them with that problem.

Eventually they were forced to release me, still unable to diagnose the obvious.

So here it is, finally, and I hope they're paying attention.

I was in the hospital because it was convenient. It was the only way to get me out of England. I was not interested in starving, killing, slashing, depriving, maiming or punishing myself.

I was dying, of course, but then we all are. Every day, in perfect increments, I was dying of loss.

The only help for my condition, then as now, is that

I refused to let go of what I loved. I wrote everything down, at first in choppy fragments; a sentence here, a few words there, it was the most I could stand at the time. Later I wrote more, my grief muffled but not eased by the passage of time.

When I go back over my writing now I can barely read it. The happiness is the worst. Some days I can't bring myself to remember. But I will not relinquish a single detail of the past. What remains of my life depends on what happened six years ago.

In my brain, in my limbs, in my dreams, it is still happening.

Two

It took all this time for the war to end.

I was going to say For Good, but even now I don't want to press my luck.

The Occupation itself lasted less than nine months; by Christmas that first year it was over. By then I was back in New York City, not because I wanted to be, but because I was half dragged and half deported and the final half was blackmail, and after all the rest of the things I managed to resist, I didn't have the strength left for that particular fight.

The worst part about those years wasn't the hospital, or the solitude, or the war, or even being away from Edmond.

It was the not knowing.

It's fashionable nowadays to talk about cramming a whole life into a few years, especially when people turn up dead at the end of it, which increasingly they do. But for me it's been the opposite. When I left

England I entered limbo. For all that time I was waiting to come home.

You think I'm exaggerating, that I should qualify my statement: I waited, yes, but I also took a job, read books, spent days in air-raid shelters, filled out rationing papers, wrote letters, stayed alive.

But the truth is that nothing distracted me from waiting.

The. Time. Simply. Passed.

First, of course, I was reunited with my family. I met my half-sister. Less than half, really. An eighth. A fiftieth.

They named her Leonora. Snub-nosed, Precious and Refreshingly Normal, which is the line Davina's been using two or three hundred times a day for over half a decade now.

I know exactly how the conversations with my father go.

'Thank heavens there are no problems with Leonora, why, *the money alone* that's been wasted on –' (meaningful nod).

And my father, looking uncomfortable, answers, 'Of course, darling,' and silently taps his knuckles against their custom-made White Canadian Birch Headboard, for luck.

I was precious at her age too.

For my father's sake, I've pretended to be nice to Leonora. Not that she cares. She assumes admiration.

Well good for her. It's a lot easier that way.

I left the bosom of my family within a few days of being discharged from the hospital. Most of the schools had closed and it was hard to see the point of education in the midst of all that death and destruction anyway, so I moved into a derelict office building near what used to be Grand Central. No one wanted to live in that neighbourhood any more, but I liked it. The sky was bigger now and except for the occasional shooting, it was quiet.

Around the corner was The New York Public Library, main branch, Forty-second and Fifth. I assumed they were desperate for staff. Everyone in that neighbourhood was. At the interview they asked me how I felt about the bomb threats and snipers and were impressed by what they took to be my courage. I was the only one who applied for the job, which may explain why they didn't seem to mind about my previous job experience. Hall monitor in a loony bin.

Day after day I attended my duties, which were virtually non-existent. It was silent in there, cavernous and empty. Some days the only people who came in were our regulars: a small band of old-fashioned primary-source freaks and Intellectual Seekers. Everyone else stayed home and used the Internet, less worried about the quality of the information than about suicide bombers. Nearly everyone got used to living without little luxuries like library books.

It was only a few months ago that there was finally a pause in the thousands of wars being waged all over the planet. Or was it one big war? I forget.

I think everyone has.

A few days after the borders between the US and England finally reopened for Casual Passage, the letter from Piper arrived. For the longest time I couldn't bring myself to read it.

For once my father's influence came in handy. He was trying to make amends, which I appreciated.

I was one of the first people they allowed to come back.

You'd laugh at the complications of my journey. From start to finish, the trip took almost a week. Of course it wasn't all travelling, there was a lot of waiting around too, but I was used to that.

When the plane finally did touch down, I half expected, half prayed, that somehow a miracle would happen and Edmond would appear at the airport, just like last time, with his cigarette and the sweet doggy tilt to his head. But how could he?

I was disappointed nonetheless.

The procedure of checking us through was complicated so I waited with the small anxious crowd, a few Americans but mostly Brits who got stuck on the wrong side of the Atlantic when borders all over the world started to close.

Our right to be in England had to be double and

triple-confirmed, with sheaves of paperwork and finger-printed identification cards in addition to the new kind of passports we'd been issued.

All the officials at the airport carried guns. But underneath their grim expressions you could detect a hint of excitement. We were almost tourists, the first anyone had seen in years. For them, we represented the end of a long, hard winter. Like daffodils. They greeted us with barely disguised relief.

When I stepped outside, the familiar smell of that rainy April day hit me so hard I felt dizzy and had to put my bag down and wait for the spell to pass.

The airport was unrecognizable from my last visit, completely overgrown with gorse and ivy and huge prehistoric-looking thistles. Just as Isaac had predicted, the landscape was happily romping away from civilization. I half expected to see stags and wild boars on the runway.

Except for a couple of army jeeps the parking lot was empty. Their owners had hacked a space in the dense scrub that now covered everything, but the clearings looked temporary. It was like landing in a wild place; I'm glad I hadn't seen the condition of the runways beforehand.

The soldier had stamped my passport FAMILY in heavy black capital letters and I checked it now for reassurance and because I liked how fierce the word looked.

I'm coming, I said silently to everything I'd left behind, and headed for the ragged bus that would take me home.

Three

While waiting for my connection out of London, I found a phone booth that worked and punched in the number Piper sent me. A man's voice I didn't recognize answered after a long time, and said no one else was there, so I left a message with my approximate time of arrival and before he hung up he paused and said, 'They are so happy you've come.'

There was no such thing as a direct route. Seven hours and two buses later I finished my final leg of the journey just outside a village that looked as if it had been deserted for a century.

The bus was early and there was no one around, but coming down the road towards me was a graceful young woman with a heavy curtain of dark hair and the most perfect pale skin I'd ever seen.

Her face lit up in a radiant smile when she saw me and then she was running and of course it was the smile that tipped me off that she was the same as ever, and then I heard the voice crying, 'Daisy!' which was exactly the same as it always had been and I tried to look at her face and connect her with the little girl I knew but my eyes were blinded by tears and I couldn't focus.

She didn't cry, you could tell from her expression she had made up her mind she wouldn't. She just looked at me with her huge solemn eyes and looked and looked like she couldn't believe what she was seeing.

'Oh, Daisy,' she said.

Just that. And then again. 'Oh, Daisy.'

I couldn't even find a voice to answer so I embraced her instead.

Eventually she pulled away and leaned down to pick up my bag.

'Everyone's desperate to see you,' she said. And then, 'We still haven't any petrol for the jeep. Shall we walk?'

Then I laughed, because what if I'd said no? And I picked up the other bag and she took my hand just as if we'd been together all along and she was still nine years old, and we walked home in the still spring sunshine alongside the flowering overgrown hedgerows, past the apple trees in blossom and the fields gone to seed, up the hill. And everything she hadn't explained well enough in her letter she told me now, about Isaac and Aunt Penn and Osbert.

Neither of us mentioned Edmond.

Here are some of the things she told me.

She told me Aunt Penn's death had finally been

confirmed two years after she first left for Oslo. I knew that. But I didn't know she'd been shot trying to re-enter the country a few months after the war started, desperate to get back to her family.

Poor sisters, I thought. Both murdered by their children.

Our war and theirs turned out to be remarkably similar. There were snipers and small groups of rebels everywhere, disorganized bands of covert fighters and half the time you couldn't tell the Good Guys from the Bad Guys and neither could they. Buses blew up, and occasionally an office building or a post office or a school, and bombs were found in shopping malls and packages, and sometimes for no reason that anyone could explain there would be a ceasefire, and then some-one somewhere would step on a landmine and we'd all be off again. You could ask a thousand people on seven continents what it was all about and you wouldn't get the same answer twice; nobody really knew for sure but you could bet one or more of the following words would crop up: oil, money, land, sanctions, democracy. The tabloids waxed nostalgic for the good old days of WWII, when The Enemy all spoke a foreign language and the army went somewhere else to fight.

And yet life went on. Although the borders remained sealed to tourists, things started returning to something a little closer to normal after the Occupation ended, which was soon after I left.

By the time it became official that Aunt Penn wasn't coming home, Osbert was eighteen, and since no one else was interested in adopting what was left of the family, it fell to him, though as Piper said, nothing much changed. 'He moved out last year,' she told me, 'to live with his girlfriend, but we still see him all the time.'

Isaac, apparently, was still Isaac. He spoke more now, but mostly to the animals. He'd spent the last five years building up the flock of tangly-haired sheep again, and he and Piper had goats, a small herd of cows, pigs, two riding horses, a pony and chickens. The vegetable gardens were huge, with a section left untouched to provide seeds for next year.

They had decided to be self-sufficient; it seemed the safest thing to be now, and the natural way for them to live. In addition to the farm, Piper said people brought Isaac livestock with a variety of physical and mental problems because they knew he could fix them and it was a luxury these days to give up on a sick or danger-ous animal. She said people in the county called him the Witch Doctor, but in a nice way.

And then she told me about herself, how she was in love with Jonathan, and how he was training to be a doctor and she wanted to be one too. The universities had opened again but the waiting list to get in was long and Piper thought she might not qualify for entry this year. I could tell by what she said that it wasn't some temporary teen romance, but what else would you expect of Piper? She told me he loved her. Well of course he did. I told her I couldn't wait to meet him and it was true.

We walked the last few hundred yards uphill in silence and as we approached the drive I could see the honey-coloured stone of the house. My hand tightened around Piper's and my heart stuttered, contracting so hard on each beat that the blood whooshed in my ears.

Isaac was there to greet us, holding a pretty Border collie by the collar.

He smiled as I hugged him close and smelled his familiar smell and saw how he had grown taller than me, and quiet and slender and strong.

'I wanted to come and collect you,' he said gravely. 'But Piper wouldn't let me. She's very possessive you know.'

I think it was the longest sentence I ever heard him speak. It was accompanied by the familiar tilt of the head and a slightly raised eyebrow and I felt the ground rush away from me, so strong was the memory, and the fear.

'Come on,' Piper said, taking hold of my hand once more. 'Let's go and see Edmond.'

Four

Six years.

My fantasies were as constant as I was: Edmond and me. Living some sort of life.

That was it. I never bothered filling in the details. The details didn't matter.

The day was warm and Edmond was outdoors, sitting carefully upright on a lawn chair in the white garden, his eyes half closed. He sat facing away from us and Piper went and knelt in front of him.

'Edmond,' she whispered, her hand resting lightly on his knee. 'Edmond, look who's come.'

He turned his head then and I couldn't even move towards him or make my face have an expression.

He was thin, much thinner than I am now, his face worn. Where Isaac was lean and graceful, he just looked gaunt.

His eyes narrowed slightly and he turned his head back away from me and closed them again. Closed the subject.

I wasn't prepared.

Piper pulled a metal folding chair over and pushed me into it and went off to make tea and at first I just looked at him and eventually he looked back with his eyes the colour of unsettled weather. His arms were covered in scars – some new, some healing over, some disappearing into thin white lines. I could see the same thin lines etched around his neck and he'd developed a nervous habit of running his fingers along the ridges over and over again.

'Edmond . . .'

I didn't know how to continue.

Not that it mattered. To him I was still thousands of miles away. The borders were still closed.

I sat there, awkward, not knowing what to do. I wanted to touch him but when he opened his eyes again the expression in them was poison.

Piper came back with the tea. Good old reliable English tea. Two World Wars ago, battlefield nurses gave cups of tea to the wounded and it leaked through their bullet holes and killed them.

I turned and looked at the garden, meticulously tended, by whom, I wondered? The child angel had been cleared of moss and planted all around with snowdrops and white narcissus that poured out an overpowering scent. I thought of the ghost of that long-dead child, watching us, its desiccated bones sunk deep into the ground below.

On the warm stone walls, climbing roses were just coming into bloom and great twisted branches of honeysuckle and clematis wrestled each other as they tumbled up and over the top of the wall. Against another wall were white apple blossoms on branches cut into sharp crucifixes and forced to lie flat against the stone. Below, the huge frilled lips of giant tulips in shades of white and cream nodded in their beds. They were almost finished now, spread open too far, splayed, exposing obscene black centres. I've never had my own garden but I suddenly recognized something in the tangle of this one that wasn't beauty. Passion, maybe. And something else. Rage.

It was Edmond, I thought. I recognized him in the plants.

I turned back and met his eyes, hard and angry and unyielding.

It was such a beautiful day. Warm and full of life. I couldn't reconcile it with this scene.

Piper looked at me and smiled a small tired smile.

'Give him time,' she said as though he couldn't hear us at all.

Well what choice did I have?

After that day, I could barely enter the garden without a huge effort of will. The air was suffocating, charged, the hungry plants sucking at the earth with their ferocious appetites. You could almost watch them grow, pressing their fat green tongues up through the black earth. They emerged selfish and starving, gasping for air.

Once inside, I couldn't breathe. I felt claustrophobic, choked, desperately thinking bright thoughts so Edmond couldn't get inside my head and know how terrified and furious and guilty I felt. But I don't think he even tried.

And still he sat there, as still and as cold as the statue of the dead child.

I sat with him for a shorter and shorter time each day as my fear took over and the grasping whiteness of the garden blinded me.

I thought of excuses, involved myself totally in the farm. There was plenty of work to do so I could fool myself that no one noticed the obvious.

It was like not eating. Everyone knew.

After a few days I found myself alone in the barn with Isaac. Piper had gone to meet Jonathan, returning from a week at the hospital. Travel was so difficult that it made sense for him to stay for long stretches without coming home.

For once Isaac looked at me directly, the way he looked at the dogs.

'Talk to him,' he said with no preface.

'I can't.'

'Why else did you come?'

'He won't listen.'

'He is listening. He can't help listening. It's what

caused all the trouble for him in the first place.'

I knew any of them would tell me the whole story but I didn't dare ask. I didn't dare know.

I looked at Isaac's eyes with their strange mix of warmth and dispassion. I could see that he suffered for Edmond as much as he could suffer for another human being.

And suddenly the thing inside that had kept me focused all these years rose in my throat like vomit. It was as strong as poison and for once I didn't fight it down or try to reshape it as something polite.

'If he's listening SO FUCKING HARD,' I shouted, 'WHY CAN'T HE HEAR THAT THE ONLY WAY I'VE MANAGED TO SURVIVE EVERY DAY FOR ALL THESE YEARS IS BECAUSE OF HIM?'

'He knows,' Isaac said. 'He's just forgotten how to believe it.'

I said nothing for a long time.

'The garden frightens me.'

'Yes,' he said.

We stared into each other's eyes and I saw what I needed to see.

'Keep telling him,' he said calmly, and then went back to feeding the pigs.

There was nothing else to do. I kept telling him. I returned to the garden and sat with him hour after hour saying it again and again, and most of the time

I could feel the doors slammed shut so he didn't have to listen. But I was determined.

LISTEN TO ME YOU BASTARD

He didn't move.

LISTEN TO ME.

In the end something happened. In the end, the warmth and the scent and the heavy slow buzz of bees seduced me, worked on my brain like opium, so the tightly clenched core of fear and fury that had sustained me all those years began to unfurl.

I began to open too.

I love you, I told him at last. And then I told him over and over, until the words no longer sounded like words.

And finally he turned to me, his eyes dull, and he spoke.

'Then why did you leave me?'

And so I tried to explain about our journey and the day Piper and I were at the house looking for him as usual and the phone ringing and my father's voice at the other end and how for all those years I wished I hadn't picked up the phone that day but I did and by the time I realized what his plan was for me there was nothing I could do because he knew where I was and he had International Connections and despite all my journeys and triumphs over adversity I was still just a fifteen-year-old kid stuck in a war, powerless in the face of an Official Medical Certificate Requiring Immediate Hospitalization. Abroad.

My father thought he was doing what was best for me.

Edmond turned his face away. Of course he knew the story. He must have heard it a hundred times from Piper.

I guess he had to hear it from me.

I leaned over and took both his hands in mine and pressed them to my face and when he tried to pull away I wouldn't let him. And then, not caring whether he was listening or not, I told him everything else. I told him about all the years reliving every second of our time together, the years trying to find him, the years of nothing and nobody else. And every minute of every year I was trying to come home.

We sat there as day turned to twilight and twilight to evening and the moon rose and the constellations moved across the sky and I talked and he listened and it took almost all night to tell him everything but I didn't stop until there was nothing left to tell. And when I finally went to let go of his hands because mine were cold and exhausted and cramped, I couldn't.

We sat like that, close together in the white garden, lit by the cold white light of the stars, with only each other for warmth.

'OK,' he said finally, and he said it out loud, his voice odd and strained, like he'd forgotten how to speak.

That was it. OK.

And then he freed his hands and took mine, stiff

and icy cold, and wrapped them in his, which were warm.

It was a start.

Five

According to Piper, after the Occupation finished most of the young men were drafted into the army and a good proportion of the urban population began to redistribute itself towards the countryside where it was supposed to be safer. Cooperatives sprang up to handle the farm work and try to keep everyone fed.

Piper met Jonathan through their cooperative; he worked with one of the doctors and she ran the milking barns. There was no need for courtship, they simply met one day and were together after that.

He lived with them now; it was Jonathan who answered my phone call from London. He and Piper made a good couple. Where she was serious and gentle he was intense and humorous, utterly engaged in the world in a way none of her family really was.

I liked him immediately. As outsiders, we both saw our role somewhere in the quadrant of Privileged Caretakers.

I knew he protected her when he could.

Jonathan told me all about the years that followed my departure. Eventually the schools reopened, farm shops sold food, distribution networks sprang up and the black market offered everything from imported drugs to new shoes if you could afford to pay.

'It's been a bad time for so many people,' he said, and Piper looked at her hands. 'So many deaths.'

'Tell me what happened,' I said finally, late one evening when the sky was striped pink and gold and the garden was lit with the last rays of the setting sun.

I knew that Edmond and Isaac had survived, but that's all I knew. I didn't know how, or what they'd seen. What they'd done.

Piper remained silent, and so it was from Jonathan that I heard the last piece of the story.

According to Jonathan, Edmond and Isaac had lived peacefully at Gateshead throughout the summer, as Piper and I had at Reston Bridge. Then things started to change. The atmosphere darkened, they heard reports of violence and unrest, and both Edmond and Isaac knew, in the way they knew things, that something was wrong, something bad was going to happen. They tried to warn people, tried to talk to Dr Jameson. He listened, was sympathetic. But he knew it would take an immense leap of faith for anyone to act. The small community was too settled and too frightened to run and hide in the woods because of something in the air and the premonitions of a couple of kids. It wasn't enough to make them leave. You can't really blame them, especially now.

Isaac knew that his first responsibility was to survive, and to make sure Edmond survived. But Edmond didn't see it that way. The way he saw it, if they left, they abandoned all those people to certain death. For the first time, they fought, and Isaac proved the stronger of the two. He turned the full force of his will on Edmond. Bullied him. He did what was required to make sure they escaped alive. And they did. But it divided them: Isaac could live with the consequences and Edmond couldn't.

They went into hiding together, but it was too dangerous. The area was swarming with soldiers and vigilantes and Isaac knew that in order to survive, they'd have to keep moving. He tried to convince Edmond to return home, but he wouldn't, or maybe he couldn't. In the end, Isaac did what he never thought was possible, and that was to leave Edmond behind. Maybe he hoped Edmond would follow him.

'Isaac hid for some time in the village.'

Jonathan looked at Piper and she looked away.

'He arrived here two days after you left.'

I gasped as if I'd been punched hard in the stomach. The things that break your heart when you think there's nothing left to break.

Jonathan took a deep breath.

'When Isaac left, Edmond went back to Gateshead, even though he knew how dangerous it was. He had worked and lived side by side with every one of those people for months and perhaps he felt that if he could warn them better, make it clearer, force them to listen – he could save them.

'Well, obviously he couldn't. He must have given up at last, escaped when he saw there was nothing more he could do.'

Jonathan shook his head. 'How all those people, including the children, would have hidden in the woods with no food . . .'

He paused.

'There were thousands of stories just like this one, and mostly they didn't end happily.'

None of us said a word.

Jonathan took another breath and continued. 'We don't know exactly what happened next, but you know what happened at Gateshead. You and Piper know better than anyone. Soon afterwards, Edmond was found a few miles away by soldiers, not our soldiers. He was half-dead with starvation and you can imagine what else. They held him for over a month but didn't harm him, except that there was never enough food and they didn't bother wasting what they had on him. We don't know why they kept him alive, they just did. In the end, they got so used to him and the fact that he never tried to move or speak or escape, that he just stood up one day and walked off. He walked home. God knows how he made it to the house, but he did, and that's where Piper and Isaac found him, sick and starving and silent. They managed to get him up to the lambing barn where they were hiding, but he wouldn't speak at all or tell them what happened. Not for –'

He looked at Piper. 'More than a year. You've seen what he's done to himself. As if he hadn't suffered, or been punished enough. And for what? For being alive, I guess.'

We didn't say anything for a long time.

Finally Piper spoke, her voice soft.

'And then there was the garden. It took a long time for him to do anything other than sit in a chair, but he started, slowly, just digging and helping with the vegetables, and still not saying much of anything, and each day he did more. It helped him, you could see how much it helped him. He weeded and pruned and dug up old bulbs and put them away for the winter, and collected seed and labelled it, and when spring came he started to plant things and not just for food – for something else.'

She looked at me.

'He'd never cared that much for the garden before, but once he started working he was compulsive, tireless. Day after day he worked until well after dark, and there was no point calling him in. He couldn't stop even if he'd wanted to.

'It was worse for him in winter, with so much less to do, but even then we'd find him out in the snow, clearing off branches so they wouldn't break and wrapping plants in sacks and hay to keep them from freezing. Sometimes his intensity was frightening, but afterwards he always seemed calmer. He's never told us about going back to Gateshead, or what happened when he was with the soldiers. We never heard from him what happened after he and Isaac split up. Jonathan found out most of it from people who saw him, who knew what was going on. He's locked it inside and this is how it comes out.'

She pointed to the dense thorny branches of a Blood Rose, cut and pinioned into cruel horizontals against the wall, yet still wild and heavy with dark red blooms. We watched a honeybee lurch from one fat flower to the next, drunk and staggering under the weight of all that botanical destiny.

And suddenly I knew something with terrifying clarity. I knew Edmond had witnessed the massacre. Seen the people murdered in cold blood, the men and women, and the children, dying, the animals murdered or left to starve. I don't know how he survived and I probably never will know, but I knew unequivocally that he was there.

I couldn't begin to imagine the effect on him. I didn't have to.

I looked at Piper. I could see in her eyes that she

didn't know. Jonathan wouldn't have guessed. As for Isaac? Doesn't he know everything that happens to any one of us?

'That's it,' Piper said. 'That's the end.'

But I knew it wasn't. They'd left out a chapter.

The one where the hero comes home to find me gone.

Six

I became a gardener, of sorts.

It was the only way to talk to him, not with words, but with hard work and the feel of old tools, and with fat bulbs buried and waiting deep in the rich soil. I watched him and learned from him, digging and planting and making things grow. At first he didn't help me, but I didn't need his help. I just needed to be there with him in the sunshine, planting tiny seeds in the crumbling earth and willing them to flower.

Now we walk, and he talks to me sometimes, tells me the names of the plants we come across in the field. They're hard to remember and there are too many of them, and the only ones I manage to keep in my head are the ones that saved my life.

Corylus avellana. Hazelnuts. *Rubus fruticosus*. Black-berries. *Agaricus campestris*. Field mushroom. *Rorippa nasturtium-aquaticum*. Watercress. *Allium ursinum*. Wild garlic. *Malus domestica*. Apples.

Sometimes we sit together the way we did a thousand

years ago and we don't say a word but just listen to the thrushes and the skylarks. He even smiles occasionally, remembering, and that's when I turn sideways and look at his face, trace his scars with my finger and without speaking I tell him again and again that I'm home.

And so, after all this time, we're together, Edmond and I.

The facts of his existence are plain. I know that he will never silence those unspeakable voices. He heard how people killed, and how they died, and their voices infected him, coursed through his body, poisoned him. He didn't know how to turn off the noise, or turn the hate back out on to the world like the rest of us. He turned it on himself. You can see that from the scars on him.

Isaac survived because he listened to animals. He could help them, which makes pain bearable. And Piper? Piper had me. By saving Piper I saved myself, and all the things that might have killed us were also the things that saved us. Saved from the ravages of war by stubbornness and ignorance and an insatiable hunger for love.

I have no idea how damaged Edmond is, I just know that he needs peace and he needs to be loved. And both those things I can do.

So now I'm here with him, and with Piper and Isaac and Jonathan and the cows and the horses and the sheep and the dogs, and the garden, and all the hard work of running a farm and staying alive in a country deformed and misshapen by war.

I know all about those conditions, only this time they're outside of me. And anyway, fighting back is what I've discovered I do best.

After all this time, I know exactly where I belong.

Here. With Edmond.

And that's how I live now.

Turn over for more brilliant writing
from Meg Rosoff.

PICTURE ME GONE

1

The first Mila was a dog. A Bedlington terrier. It helps if you know these things. I'm not at all resentful at being named after a dog. In fact, I can imagine the scene exactly. *Mila*, my father would have said, that's a nice name. Forgetting where he'd heard it. And then my mother would remember the dog and ask if he was absolutely sure, and when he didn't answer, she would say, OK, then. Mila. And then looking at me think, Mila, my Mila.

I don't believe in reincarnation. It seems unlikely that I've inherited the soul of my grandfather's long-dead dog. But certain traits make me wonder. Was it entirely coincidence that Mila entered my father's head on the morning of my birth? Observing his daughter, one minute old, he thought first of the dog, Mila? Why?

My father and I are preparing for a journey to New York, to visit his oldest friend. But yesterday things changed. His friend's wife phoned to say he'd left home.

Left home? Gil asks. What on earth do you mean?

Disappeared, she says. No note. Nothing.

Gil looks confused. Nothing?

You'll still come? says the wife.

And when Gil is silent for a moment, thinking it through, she says, Please.

Yes, of course, Gil says, and slowly replaces the phone in its cradle.

He'll be back, Gil tells Marieka. He's just gone off by himself to think for a while. You know what he's like.

But why now? My mother is puzzled. When he knew you were coming? The timing is . . . peculiar.

Gil shrugs. By this time tomorrow he'll be back. I'm certain he will.

Marieka makes a doubtful noise but from where I'm crouched I can't see her face. What about Mila? she says.

A few things I know: It is Easter holiday and I am out of school. My mother is working all week in Holland and I cannot stay at home alone. My father lives inside his head and it is better for him to have company when he travels, to keep him on track. The tickets were bought two months ago.

We will both still go.

I enjoy my father's company and we make a good pair. Like my namesake, Mila the dog, I have a keen awareness of where I am and what I'm doing at all times. I am not given to dreaminess, have something of a terrier's determination. If there is something to notice, I will notice it first.

I am good at solving puzzles.

My packing is nearly finished when Marieka comes to say that she and Gil have decided I should still go. I am already arranging clues in my head, thinking through the possibilities, looking for a theory.

I have met my father's friend sometime in the distant past but I don't remember him. He is a legend in our family for

2

once saving Gil's life. Without Matthew there would be no me. For this, I would like to thank him, though I never really get the chance.

It seems so long ago that we left London. Back then I was a child.

I am still, technically speaking, a child.

He just wanted a decent book to read ...

Not too much to ask, is it? It was in 1935 when Allen Lane, Managing Director of Bodley Head Publishers, stood on a platform at Exeter railway station looking for something good to read on his journey back to London. His choice was limited to popular magazines and poor-quality paperbacks – the same choice faced every day by the vast majority of readers, few of whom could afford hardbacks. Lane's disappointment and subsequent anger at the range of books generally available led him to found a company – and change the world.

'We believed in the existence in this country of a vast reading public for intelligent books at a low price, and staked everything on it'
Sir Allen Lane, 1902–1970, founder of Penguin Books

The quality paperback had arrived – and not just in bookshops. Lane was adamant that his Penguins should appear in chain stores and tobacconists, and should cost no more than a packet of cigarettes.

Reading habits (and cigarette prices) have changed since 1935, but Penguin still believes in publishing the best books for everybody to enjoy. We still believe that good design costs no more than bad design, and we still believe that quality books published passionately and responsibly make the world a better place.

So wherever you see the little bird – whether it's on a piece of prize-winning literary fiction or a celebrity autobiography, political tour de force or historical masterpiece, a serial-killer thriller, reference book, world classic or a piece of pure escapism – you can bet that it represents the very best that the genre has to offer.

Whatever you like to read – trust Penguin.